Angel of Blood

A Hellfire Novella Book One

Hayley Briana

Copyright © 2023 by Hayley Briana
All rights reserved. No part of this publication may be reproduced, stored, or transmitted in any form or by any means, electronic, mechanical, photocopying, recording, scanning, or otherwise, without written permission from the publisher. It is illegal to copy this book, post it to a website, or distribute it by any other means without permission.

<u>DON'T BE A DICK WHO STEALS FROM AUTHORS!</u>

This novel is entirely a work of fiction. The names, characters, and incidents portrayed in it are the work of the author's imagination. Any resemblance to actual persons, living or dead, events or localities is entirely coincidental.

Hayley Briana asserts the moral right to be identified as the author of this work.

First Edition

ISBN: 979-8-9874871-1-2

Cover Art by Hayley Briana
Formating by Hayley Briana

<u>YOU CAN</u>
<u>REPORT PIRATING</u>

Not many people are aware, but if you notice
pirating of an author's work (or any pirating in general)
you can report it anonymously to the FBI.
As we have seen, they can take down a site for pirating.

Supporting these institutions makes you a thief.
NO ONE IS ENTITLED TO SOMEONE ELSE'S WORK!
Pirating is a crime and you can face large fines of
up to $250,000 USD and jail time of 5 years.

If you can't afford the book(s) maybe try reaching out
to the author directly. Many are willing to offer you a free
download of their book.
Also, joining an author's newsletter is a great way to
stay up to date on any sales or freebies they have offered.

**To report pirating you can contact your local
FBI Office and/or report online at
https://www.ic3.gov/ or https://tips.fbi.gov/**

For the kinky baddies who love a bit of blood and revenge with their romance.

CONTENT WARNING

Disclaimer: This book contains explicit content and dark themes that may be considered traumatic and offensive to some readers.
Please check triggers before reading.
If you are uncomfortable with some of these topics please put this book down and do not read it.
This work of adult fiction is only for those 18 or older.

For a complete list of triggers
please visit HayleyBrianaWrites.com

Scan to see a list of triggers

Playlist

Rest in Peace - Dorothy

God Sent Me as Karma - Emlyn

Spider in the Roses - Sonia Leigh

Alpha - Little Destroyer

Killer - Valerie Broussard

Horns - Bryce Fox

Killer Queen - Mad Tsai

Toxic - 2WEI

The Death of Peace of Mind - Bad Omens

Hellfire - Barns Courtney

Big Bad Wolf - Roses & Revolutions

Table of Contents

PROLOGUE

"I'm not here to forgive you. Only your god can forgive you for the darkness of your soul."

Those were the last words he heard as the bullet met its mark between his eyes. His vacant eyes watched me as he crumbled to the floor. Another name off the list, and soon my ledger would drip red with their blood. I wouldn't stop until I had my revenge.

All that could be heard in this lonely church was the rain cascading down the stained-glass windows and the clack of my heels as I disappeared into the chilled night.

Onto the next, and last, target.

CHAPTER ONE

Angel

I was sitting on the fire escape of my crappy studio apartment. The rain was still coming down, but I just didn't care. I only had one last person to kill to avenge Jessica and he would be the hardest to get to. Especially with the other three dead and found murdered.

I tried to block out the memories that kept assaulting me tonight. You'd think it would be the fact I'd murdered someone in cold blood, but no. It was simply the face of Jessica with her fair skin and red hair laying in a heap, surrounded by a puddle of her own blood. Her face frozen in the terror of her last moments. All I could see was how her dress had been ripped from her body, hanging in tattered and bloody strips from her limbs. I wished all I could see was her beauty. Instead, I was haunted by that last image of her. When I found her dead in our home.

I was her older sister by two years. After we got out of the system, I failed her. Spending my life protecting her had taken a back seat. To give her a life I thought she deserved, I had been trying to earn enough for us to live comfortably. Working two jobs at the time hadn't been ideal, but someone needed to take care of her. She wanted to go to school, so I gave her that opportunity without the added worry of how to pay for it on top of our other bills. I should have paid more attention. I should have seen the signs and known when she started hanging around the less unsavory individuals at her school, especially at eighteen. They were the sort of people you didn't want to notice your existence, but she thrived on their attention. The bad boys loved her innocence. Someone who was easy to manipulate. She quickly became their favorite toy. I knew they were low-ranking members of the crew that ran the city. It soon became apparent that she was working her way up the ranks when she started bringing home expensive gifts. There was no way she could have afforded it on her own. I should have warned her, said something, but I was just too busy trying to keep the bills paid and her taken care of. I never thought I'd find her dead in our living room eight years ago.

I knew exactly who had been responsible for her death the day I found her. Previously, I'd scrounged up enough money to put a video security system in the house in case something were to happen. The footage showed every moment of what they'd done to her. The five men who pinned her to the ground as she tried to fight them off. How they'd torn her clothes to get to her and took turns forcing themselves on her. It hadn't mattered what part of her they had sunk their dicks into. All they cared about was taking from her and when they were done, her "boyfriend" stood up and put a bullet in her head. I'm sure it was over some petty jealously that she'd been fucking around on him, but that didn't warrant what they'd done to her.

The cops hadn't done shit, even though I had the evidence of what had occurred. They had the police department in their pocket, so nothing stuck. So it left me on my own to mourn the loss of my sister. I'd get justice for her if it was the last thing I did.

"Just one more Jessica. Those old bastards will get what they deserve." I whispered to the darkened sky before climbing back into my window.

I needed to get this blood washed off of me and get ready for surveillance by the next day. Jonathan, the little fucker I'd just killed in a church, had told me everything I needed to know to find his boss. I knew where

I could find him now and how I was going to get close to him. Using his business against him, I was determined to catch his eye. Madax Ashford would regret the day he ever laid eyes on my sister.

I parked outside of the Hellfire club and watched as the line continued to grow outside. It was the hottest club in town, even though the majority didn't realize it was a front for the mafia that ran this city. It was owned by the boss's youngest son, Damon, and they had most of their underground meetings here. How the place had a clean record, I had no clue. The first thing I needed to do was get into the club, then I could work on the details of the plan to take down Madax.

Taking a deep breath, I climbed out of my black, beat-up 69 impala, adjusted my short dress, and made my way to the entrance. In this dress, I left little to the imagination, which would come in handy with the bouncer manning the door. It would grab the attention of most men if I set my sights on them. It was black, short, strapless showing off the ink covering my body. I had paired it with the tallest strappy red heels I'd ever owned. God, I hated this outfit. I hated the way heads turned as I approached the bouncer and as said man glanced my way; I gave him the most seductive smile I could muster.

"Sorry, beautiful, you'll have to wait in line like everyone else tonight." He said in a deep voice that sounded like he smoked three packs a day. He appeared fairly young, probably in his mid to late thirties, with the build of a lifter, a shaved head, and honey eyes. I could tell right away he used to be in the military.

"Oh, come on handsome, it can be our secret," I said to him, trailing my manicured nails up his muscular chest, "I can make it worth your while."

He seemed to contemplate for only a moment before going back to being stoic, "No can do. You'll have to wait in line like the others."

God, why couldn't he just make getting in easier for me? I forced myself to pout and run my eyes down his body. "Well, I guess it's your loss."

As I moved away from him to take a place in line outside the club, I heard the sexiest, deep tenor I'd ever had the pleasure of hearing, speaking from inside the door, "Ray, let her through."

I glanced over to see who had spoken and my breath caught. This man I recognized from my research and he could work to get what I wanted. Damon Ashford.

The mafia prince himself was standing at the door in all his god-like glory. No man should ever look and sound like he did. He was at least 6'2", muscular in all the right places, covered in ink, with a well-groomed beard, long brown hair tied up into a messy bun, and steel-blue eyes that could bring any woman to her knees. He was bad news and could be a real problem if I didn't play my cards right.

I smiled his way, flipping my long, midnight hair over my shoulder, and sauntered up to him, "And who might I thank for saving me from waiting out in the cold?"

He flashed me a crooked smirk while lighting a cigarette. "Names Damon, and you?"

"Angel."

He let his steel eyes trail down my body and I could swear I felt the heat from his gaze like a caress. He was definitely going to be a problem. With a single glance, he could set my skin ablaze.

He puffed out a ring of smoke as his eyes met mine again and extended his arm to me. "Angel," He paused like he was savoring my name on his tongue, "let me buy you a drink."

It wasn't a question, and I didn't like the fact he thought he could boss me around. I fought the urge to glare at him and opted to simply smile up at him as he towered over me. "It would be my pleasure."

He finished his smoke and tossed the butt into a nearby ashtray before offering me his arm. I guess it was a plus that he didn't throw the damn things on the ground like most idiots. I timidly slipped my arm into his and let him escort me into the already packed club. Once we walked through the interior doors, I became slightly overwhelmed by the loud trap music and the smell of booze, smoke, and sweat. The neon and strobe lights were the only light within the entire club, other than those that lined the bar set against the sidewall as you entered the club. If Damon weren't escorting me, I probably would have spent most of the night searching for any sign of Madax in this damned crowd.

Damon led us straight to the bar and waved the bartender over.

"Damon, what can I get for you, sir?" The young man in his early twenties asked. He was blonde with a long, faded haircut. The top was long enough that the lengths fell over one of his green eyes. He was attractive and I could tell he used that to his advantage working in this club. Women were eyeing him almost as much as Damon. What was with the men who worked here being so attractive?

"Scotch, Zack," He said to the bartender before leaning in to whisper in my ear, "and you Angel?"

I felt myself shiver as his breath brushed my ear and neck. "Pomegranate martini, please."

Fuck, why was I having this reaction to a man I didn't know a thing about outside of his name and who his father was? He was the son of my target, and I needed to get my shit together. I needed to get away from him so I could do the job I set out to do. He ordered my drink and Zack got to work, making them as quickly as possible. Once he finished, he handed the drinks to Damon, who nodded for me to follow him through the crowd. He led me over to an empty plush sectional off to the side of the dance floor. He sat down, placing my drink on the table, leaned back, and crossed his ankle over the opposite knee.

I guess I would have to play nice for a bit. I took a seat next to him, maintaining a comfortable distance between us. Before crossing my legs, I grabbed my drink from the table, relaxing into the plush cushions.

"Thank you for getting me in and for the drink," I say politely while scanning the dance floor, acting as if I was looking for someone. I was hoping I would see Madax.

"My pleasure. Are you meeting someone here tonight?" He asks in a lazy tone.

"Just a few friends." I lie smoothly, glancing back over at him. "Why did you vouch to get me into the club?"

I needed to know what game he was playing, so I knew how I needed to proceed with this chance meeting.

"By the way you were sweet-talking the guy out front you seemed… desperate." He seemed to contemplate that last word.

I couldn't control my reaction to that comment and glared directly at him. "I've never been desperate for a day in my life."

Before he could reply, I stood and smiled in his direction. "Thanks again for the drink." I spoke in a clipped voice and walked away. I didn't have time to play with him when there was a much bigger fish to fry.

I spent the night wandering in the shadows of the club. Keeping an eye out for any sign of Madax. I had a feeling he was keeping to the upper levels, where I could see a mirrored wall above the dance floor. I confirmed my suspicion when a group of businessmen were escorted upstairs. Deciding that this wouldn't pan out the way I had planned, I would need to find a different way in. I finished my drink and made my way back to the bar. I waited to be served and smiled when Zack glanced my way. He smoothly slid a customer's drink across the bar to them before walking over to me.

"Another one for you, beautiful?" He smirked, taking my empty glass.

"Not this time, Zack, but you could tell a girl how she gets a job in a place like this," I said, giving him my most flirtatious smile.

"Oh, that's easy and as it just so happens, we are currently looking for a waitress. I'm in charge of the bar so I can hire you," he said with a wink. "Think you could start on Monday?"

"Monday would work out perfectly." Damn, that was much easier than I thought it would be. I could see just a hint of mischief in his gaze, so I knew that there had to be an ulterior motive for hiring me without so much as an interview.

Zack told me all the details of when to show up and that we can go over training before the weekend hits. I thanked him for the opportunity; we exchanged contact information, and I quickly slipped out of the club. Now that I had a way to get into the club regularly, I also had a way to get close to the bastard who killed my sister.

CHAPTER TWO

Damon

I watched as the little Angel wandered off to disappear into the crowd with a confident grin. I had a gut feeling that she was hiding something, and I wanted to know what it was. It had been a while since anyone had caught my interest.

Once I'd lost sight of her in the crowd, I stood from my spot and made my way to the VIP section on the upper level of the club. The guards let me in and the room immediately became quiet when the door shut behind me. It was a soundproofed room that housed a private bar and sitting area. The far wall overlooked the club with a floor-to-ceiling window, which I silently walked over to and glanced out. Looking for a certain dark-haired beauty.

My father was sitting on the couch with a phone to his ear, discussing a new business deal. Who knew what about at this point? He had his fingers in every dirty pot in the city; from drugs to the skin trade. I had never been a fan of all his methods for running the business. The old fuck needed to just give Dimitri control because he was fucking up the reputation of the family name.

He hung up the phone and walked over next to me. I could smell his expensive cologne and it made me sick. Like he was trying to cover up the rot inside of him despite being in excellent health, sadly.

"How are things on the ground tonight?" He asked as he took a swig from his tumbler.

"Things are fine. No fights have broken out, and the bar is running smoothly. I'm still looking for someone to help with the bar. It's far too busy for just Zack and Cherry. How's *business*?"

He glanced my way from the corner of his eye, but I paid him no mind. "Expanding."

That could only mean that the call was about finding new "recruits" for the skin trade. It was the one part of the business that none of us ever agreed on. Even Dimitri hated it. Regardless of the money it brought in, once Dimitri and I took over, it would be the first thing to go. We may run the city and it's underground, but that was a level of debauchery I would never sink to.

"Go enjoy yourself tonight, son. I have no use for you this evening." He spoke with authority as he walked over to the private bar to refill his glass.

It was his way of dismissing me prior to his associates showing up. They planned to discuss using the club as a front to find more girls to fill their empty slots for market. Just the thought had me wanting to blow his brains across the wall. This was my bar, but until he was out of the picture, I had to follow orders. I'd soon kill this fucker, and those he did business with. He trained me to be a ruthless killer and I would enjoy the day I got to be his executioner.

I nodded in his direction, "Yes, sir," and walked out of the stuffy room.

I would much rather find Angel. She was going to be a fun little distraction. I wanted to see just how dark she could get. I'd leave Dimitri to deal with our father for the evening.

Making my way around the club, it disappointed me to not find a single glimpse of Angel, so I went straight to the heart of gossip, Zack. He was sliding drinks from one end of the bar to the other. How he and Cherry handled that bar alone, I would never understand. I slipped behind the bar and got to work helping him trim the herd down so that we could speak.

Once there were only a handful of people left at the bar, Zack turned to me with a raised brow, wiping his hands on a towel.

"What's up boss?" He was always so easygoing and to the point.

"Have you seen the girl I came in with earlier?" I asked as I wiped up the bar top.

"Oh, you mean Angel? Yeah, she swung back by the bar about 10 minutes ago before she left. Was asking about getting a job, so I hired her on as a waitress."

I couldn't help but grin in his direction. Of course, he'd just hire a pretty girl with no questions asked. I adored the fucker, but he had a tendency to get himself into trouble with the ladies. This did, however, make it much easier to track her down.

"When will she be starting?" I tossed the dirty towel into the wastebasket and poured myself another drink.

"Monday. Figured I'd show her the ropes before throwing her to the wolves during the weekend rush." He said, leaning against the bar, his eyes roaming across the busy floor. The horny bastard was probably looking for his next conquest.

"Sounds good." I downed my tumbler and walked off, giving him a slight wave of thanks.

CHAPTER THREE

The weekend came and went. Today was officially my first day working at the club. I opted for a casual look of a black cut-up tee that showed off just the right amount of cleavage, short daisy dukes, and thigh-high combat boots with my hair pulled up in a loose ponytail. I quickly lined my eyes in a black liner that smudged slightly, giving a not-so-put-together smokey eye, some simple mascara, and topped it off with a bold, red lip stain. Checking to make sure I had my phone and keys, and slipped my needlepoint knife into the side of my boot before heading out to the club.

Because it was a Monday afternoon, the bar was mostly empty outside of some staff and vendors. Zack waved me over when he saw me walk inside. He was sitting at the bar eating a bowl of peanuts, while Damon was standing next to him signing the paperwork of a vendor. I smiled and made my way over.

Before coming in, I looked up all I could about the club. Damon was the owner of the place and he had built it from the ground up two years ago at age 36. His father and brother were big investors in the club and did most of their business here. It was a hot spot for club-goers on the weekend and had been kept squeaky clean, at least to the eyes of the public.

Damon watched me closely as I made my way over to them, and I simply smiled as I took a seat next to Zack. I turned away from him and started talking with Zack about all the duties I'd have, the hours to expect, and just the basics of starting a new job. He even went as far as demanding that I understand that the door to the basement in the back was completely off-limits to anyone who wasn't management. Once he finished explaining everything, he gave me an apron and put me to work behind the bar, making a variety of drinks to test my skills. He watched me closely as he tossed peanuts into his mouth.

"Boss, I think we have a natural on our hands." He said, turning to Damon.

"Appears so, make me a Blue Blazer, if you will." Damon had a challenge in his eyes and it was obvious why. A Blue Blazer could be a complicated drink. I was learning, however, that the man before me was a lover of scotch.

"Coming right up, Mr. Ashford," I said, getting to work boiling some water and placing two glass mugs inside.

"Come on, man, you just have to test her with the fancy stuff, don't you?" I heard Zack say to Damon with a hint of worry in his voice.

Once the glasses were heated, I tossed the water and boiled the additional water I'd need. Laying a damp hand towel on the bar, I got to work mixing the new boiled water, scotch, and sugar into one mug. Lighting a match, I was careful to ignite the mixture, and transfer it from cup to cup before evening out both mugs, and extinguishing the flames. I topped each glass with a lemon twist. Sliding the drinks over to Damon and Zack, I flashed them a proud smile and waited for the final verdict.

They shared a silent glance before taking a swig from their mugs.

"Holy shit, this is good." Zack praised while taking another drink.

Damon eyed me as he swished the drink in the mug. I swear those steel eyes could see right through me, and I knew I'd have to be careful around him. It was obvious I intrigued him, although he didn't trust me. It's a good thing he wasn't the one I was after.

"Good start, Angel, but let's see how you do under pressure when the club's packed." He gave a crooked smirk before walking off. I couldn't help but watch him as he left. He had a nice firm ass and his muscles strained against his tight-fitted gray t-shirt. He was a god among men and I'd have had to be blind not to stare.

"Just ignore him. He's an asshole most of the time." Zack said, handing me back his empty mug and peanut bowl.

I went about cleaning up my area and washing the few dirty dishes. "He doesn't seem too bad."

"You say that now. Just wait until you get to know him better." A smirk graced his lips, and I had a feeling he wanted me to get to know our boss *much* better. Was that his plan all along?

About the time I finished cleaning up, a blonde girl with a bubbly personality skipped up to the bar and sat next to Zack.

"Hey Zacky! Is this the new girl? Hi, it's nice to meet you. I'm Cherry, the only other waitress in this place." She giggled. Though she was peppy, I could tell I'd enjoy working with her.

"Names Angel. It's a pleasure to meet you, Cherry." I smiled her way as I put away all the clean supplies.

Cherry and Zack showed me the ropes of everything I'd be doing once the bar opened and we spent the day getting ready for the evening crowd. They assured me that weeknights would be slow and then Friday things would get a lot more chaotic. I just hoped that this work would pay off in the end.

The week at the club flew by and I found that not once had I seen any of the Ashford family. To say it disappointed me was an understatement, but hopefully, they would show up this weekend. Most of the club running seemed to be left to Zack during the slow weeks. I got ready in my usual attire that had just become my normal, only topping it off with a black leather jacket to fight off the autumn evening chill before heading out to my night shift at the club.

I waved to Ray on my way into the club and he gave me a slight nod, as had become the norm during my first week. I came to learn a lot about the little staff of the Hellfire Club. There were very few of us. Zack was 23 and had been working here alongside his twin sister Chery since they had turned 21. Apparently, they had been family friends of the Ashford boys their entire lives and when Damon built the club; he asked them to work for him to help run the place. Ray was the quiet, broody type and was an ex-marine. I got the vibe that he had, had his hands bloodied on many accounts, and didn't want to be on his bad side. He kept his head shaved with just a slight bit of stubble along his square jaw. He was only a few years younger than Damon, and they had grown up together as well. It was more of a family dynamic and I was going to have to play it safe to stay on everyone's good side while I snooped around.

They weren't kidding about the club turning to chaos on Friday. Only thirty minutes into making it in for my shift, the club was packed full while trap music blasted through the speakers. The dance floor was covered in sweaty bodies grinding against one another while I slipped around the crowd, taking orders and delivering drinks. The night was a blur of work and at about midnight I was beat. I placed some dirty glasses in the sink behind the bar and got to washing everything.

"Hey Angel, after you finish that, head upstairs and take a break. You've been working your ass off tonight." Zack said, giving me a wink.

"I don't know how you and Cherry handled all this on your own. It's a madhouse."

He shrugged. "It keeps you busy, and you get used to it."

I finished drying the dishes and putting them away before heading off to the break room on the top floor. The best part, it was right next to the private VIP lounge where I knew the Ashfords had most of their *business meetings*. I had seen Damon, Madax, and a tall man in a suit enter that room at the start of the night. To my surprise, as I made my way to the break room, the door wasn't guarded and had been left open a crack. I slipped up next to it to listen to the conversation going on inside.

"I don't give a shit what you two think. This is my business, and it's time you both learned your place. You don't have control of the business *yet*." A gruff voice shouted. It was aged, so I knew it had to be Madax.

"We simply don't think that market is a good look for business, sir." A calm voice, dripping with authority, spoke. That had to be the man in the suit I'd seen, the oldest Ashford son, Dimitri.

"It's good money and it'll give us more pull in other business ventures. It's already decided and I won't hear another word against it."

I heard Damon's deep scoff. He obviously wasn't happy with the choice of whatever "market" was. I decided now wasn't the best time to be snooping and slipped away, heading into the break room. I quickly made myself a cup of coffee and relaxed on the little couch for a bit, scrolling through my phone. So far, working here has not given me much to go on. I'd need to gain these people's trust so that I could get closer to Madax. It seemed the only people that could get close were his sons, his business associates who visited the club, and Cherry, on occasions when she would take drinks up to the VIP lounge and quickly be dismissed.

The door to the break room swung open, hitting the doorjamb with a loud thud. I glanced over to see Damon stomp in like he was pissed at the world. He didn't even pay me any mind as he walked over to the counter to make himself a cup of coffee.

"Bad night, boss?" I asked, going back to scrolling on my phone.

"Same shit, different day. Why are you up here instead of working?" He said, leaning against the counters and taking a sip of his coffee. Tonight, he was in a black button-up dress shirt that had 3 top buttons undone at the top, black dress slacks, shiny leather oxford shoes, and his long hair tied up in a messy bun. Fuck, it should be illegal to look that good.

"Things slowed down a bit, so Zack told me to come take a break." I glanced back his way and admired how his chest tattoos peeked out from the gap of his shirt. How I'd like to run my tongue along those designs. I'd never laid eyes on a more attractive man in my life. I had to slap myself mentally to get my head straight. He's the fucking enemy and I wouldn't let him get in my way of revenge.

He seemed to watch me just as intently as his eyes ran along my exposed legs. We continued to sit in silence, just taking each other in until he finally spoke again. "I get the feeling you are hiding something, little Angel."

I scoffed, standing up to wash my mug in the sink next to him. "Isn't everyone hiding something?"

"Fair point."

Standing this close to him, his scent filled my senses, and I squeezed my thighs together, heat pooling at my core. It was a heady mix of mahogany with a hint of something sweet, likc apples. What the fuck was wrong with me when he was around? It was this insane pull that I was helpless to resist and it did nothing except piss me off and leave me feeling distracted. I quickly washed my cup and sat it to the side of the dish drainer.

As soon as I'd placed the cup down, a hand wrapped around the front of my throat and pinned me to the wall next to the sink. I gasped in surprise and slipped my knife out of my boot, holding it to Damon's throat as he pinned me. He just smirked down at me, his blue eyes shining with a warning.

"I wouldn't do that if I were you, Angel." He said in his smooth, deep voice. I could feel his breath on my face with a hint of cigarette smoke and scotch.

I bared my teeth at him, pressing the knife harder against his throat. "Then I suggest you get your hands off me."

"And I suggest you keep your nose out of other people's business." Shit, he knew I had been spying on them.

He released my throat, backing away, and I slipped my knife back into my boot. I felt his eyes watching my every move, and it set my skin on fire. He was so much more observant than I gave him credit for. I needed to get done with this job and scatter as quickly as possible.

"Back to work. I hope the rest of your night goes better." I said, walking out without glancing his way.

CHAPTER FOUR

Damon

Sitting in this room with my father and Dimitri was the last place I wanted to be. Father was going on about how he was going to use the club to find fresh recruits for his business partner, and it was pissing me off. Like hell, if he was going to get away with fucking with my club. Dimitri sat on the sofa next to me, running his hands through his hair. A habit he had for whenever he was feeling stressed or frustrated. We were on the same page as far as my father working with the skin trade.

I sat silently, knowing that if I went off, I'd put a bullet in the old fuck's head. Glancing towards the door, I saw a head of black hair slip by the gap in the door. It seemed the little angel was a nosy little thing.

"I'd rather not have that sort of *business* around my club. I've done my best to keep this a legitimate club outside of you meeting your people here." I meant for the statement to come out calm, but I wasn't Dimitri, and it sounded more like a growl even to my own ears.

Father's glare turned directly to me as his face turned a slightly darker shade of red. "You wouldn't have this dump if it wasn't for me. I let you build it because I thought giving you something to focus on would keep you from fucking up the business. I'll do with this building as I see fit."

I clenched my fist, ready to jump off the couch and pummel the old man. Before I could inch forward off the couch, Dimitri placed a calming hand on my shoulder. The bastard knew that the old man would deserve it and he was still holding me back. I guess that was why he was the brains and knew how to handle our father in his own element. I'd always been the troublemaker who got into fights, while Dimitri was always calm and strategized every single move he made. Sometimes I was envious of his calm, like right now.

"We understand where you are coming from, sir, but Damon has worked hard to build this place up and it brings in a large percentage of our profits. However, Damon makes a fair point that this is a clean business. Maybe it would be best that your partners scout out the club for potential stock, but they follow them to an off-site location. This ensures they get what they want and Damon's business can't be tied to the girl's disappearances." Dimitri spoke fluidly with a matter-of-fact air about him. It still pissed me off that the shitbag thought he could just use my club whenever he wanted. Fuck him and fuck this.

"That seems reasonable. I will let my associates know the details."

At that, I got up and stormed out, heading to the break room in the next room. All I wanted to do was break something or make someone bleed. When was Dimitri going to give me the okay to kill the old fucker already? I know he was doing things behind the scenes, but I was tired of waiting around. I slung open the door to the break room and was surprised to see Angel laying on the couch on her phone. She glanced my way, and I pretended not to notice her as I made my way over to the coffeemaker to pour myself a cup.

"Bad night, boss?" Her soft, husky voice asked from behind me. The sound was like fucking music to my ears.

"Same shit, different day. Why are you up here instead of working?" I asked, despite knowing she hadn't had a break all evening. The club was packed, and it was her first-weekend shift.

She seemed to have a hard time keeping her eyes in one place, glancing between me and her phone as I leaned back against the countertop. I watched her face as her eyes roamed my body, setting me on fire with her scorching blue eyes. So cold they burned like ice.

"Things slowed down a bit, so Zack told me to come take a break." She said in the most seductively sweet voice I'd ever heard. I had a feeling she didn't even have to try getting a man's attention with a body and voice like that. I hadn't paid it much mind, but the girl was covered in ink. It covered every exposed area of skin I could see and, from the looks of it, they disappeared into much more interesting places. Thorny rose vines were wrapping up both her legs while snakes slithered up each one hidden in the foliage, heading in the direction I'd love to trail my hands.

We stayed silent as we both took each other in until I spoke. "I get the feeling you are hiding something, little Angel."

She scoffed, and I had to hide my grin behind my coffee mug as she stood, walking over to the sink next to me to wash out her empty cup. "Isn't everyone hiding something?"

This woman was much more observant than I gave her credit for. I knew she was sticking around for something. I just needed to find out what. Thankfully, a guy owed me a favor and was looking into her, "Fair point."

I eyed her tense figure as she washed her cup. Standing this close, I could just make out the faint scent of lavender and lilac, which seemed to draw me into her like a fly caught in a web. I wanted to bend her over this counter and fuck her wet cunt. I was positive she'd be soaking wet for me. She placed her cup in the drainer and I immediately wrapped my hand around her throat, forcing her against the wall. What I didn't expect was her holding a knife to my throat in the same instant, her back hit the wall. I couldn't help the sensation that raced through me as I grinned at her, my dick straining against the zipper of my pants. This bitch had a fire in her and I wanted to watch it burn. To let it consume me.

"I wouldn't do that if I were you," I said as she pressed the blade harder against my throat, just enough to let me know she was serious, but not to draw blood.

She bared her teeth at me like a caged animal, and a fire ignited behind those blue eyes. "Then I suggest you get your hands off me."

I grinned, knowing just how I could get her flustered. "And I suggest you keep your nose out of other people's business."

Her eyes rounded in shock and I could feel her heartbeat skyrocket along my fingers that wrapped around her throat and what a pretty throat it was, too. I had a feeling Angel would love being choked while I fucked her. She wasn't scared to fight back, which made me positive she'd be just as vicious in the sack.

I released her throat and backed away from her. Giving her some space before I took her right here in this room, whether she wanted it or not. I watched as she slipped her knife back into her boot before she straightened. She wouldn't even meet my eyes now.

"Back to work. I hope the rest of your night goes better." She said, walking out of the room without looking back.

I would most definitely be having a better night because I fully intended to end my night between those gorgeous thighs of hers. Until then, though, I needed to take care of my issue before heading back to get more business taken care of.

As quickly as I could, I shut and locked the door before undoing my pants. I was rock hard and throbbing for Angel. I wrapped my hand around the length and envisioned it was her mouth sliding along my cock. With the image of her on her knees before me and my hand creating a fast pace, I pleasured myself to the image that would be burned into my brain. Fuck her and my reaction to her. Still, I growled out her name as my release coated my hand. I couldn't wait to claim my little angel.

Hellfire had just closed, and the crew was cleaning up after a successful evening. I had slipped off to my office in the back of the club to get some last-minute paperwork done when my cell began vibrating in my pocket. I quickly fished it out, glancing at the restricted number that popped up.

"What do you have for me, Jensen?" I said, setting the paperwork to the side.

"Angel Hart, 28, was placed into the system with her younger sister at age 11. Once aging out, she took on the role of guardian for her sister, Jessica. They moved here into a small apartment 8 years ago until her sister was found murdered in their home. There were no leads, and it was labeled a cold case. Looks like someone did a marvelous job of covering shit up, you know, besides leaving the body. Since then, she's been holding odd jobs throughout the city and never seems to stay in the same place for long. She has no other records and little else is known about her. I can do some more digging if it is needed."

"Did the sister have the same last name?" I asked, lighting a cigarette and leaning back in my chair.

I heard the stroke of keys over the line before Jensen spoke again. "Jessica Murphy. Their mother was a common hooker, so they had different fathers. The fathers were never a part of their lives and their mother died from a drug overdose."

Well, that was an interesting turn of events. I recall a girl named Jessica being brought around with my father. She was young and impressionable. I wasn't sure what had happened when she just stopped showing up. The fact she had been murdered gave me a pretty good idea that my father had been involved. Was that why Angel was here? This could come in handy, if so. She could be an important part of our plans to get rid of the old fuck and take over the business.

"Thanks, Jensen," I said, hanging up the phone before he could even reply.

Standing from behind my desk, I decided on going out back to give Dimitri a call. I needed his opinion on if I should confront her. He would be much more level-headed than me. I slipped out the back door while dialing his number. When he answered, I gave him the rundown of the information Jensen had pulled up on her.

"She could be useful if it's not a coincidence that she's now working at your club. We could have her do the dirty work and we keep our hands clean," He sighed into the receiver before continuing, "Some of Father's more unsavory business partners have been reported murdered. There is no evidence or connection between them. I doubt that one woman could have taken them all out."

I grinned around my cigarette and recalled her holding that knife to my throat. "I think she might surprise you, brother."

"You find out more about her and we can go from there." I could almost hear the eye roll in his voice before he disconnected the call.

I leaned against the rough brick in the shadows, tossing my cigarette onto the pavement, when the back door to the club opened and out walked Angel with a bag of trash. I watched from the shadows as she tossed the bag into the dumpster, before walking back towards the door. However, I didn't intend on her making it that far just yet.

CHAPTER FIVE

Angel

It had been a long night. Not only had it been busy, but the encounter with Damon had been on my mind for most of the evening. I couldn't get rid of the tingling sensation of his hand on my throat. I was just ready to get home at this point. Walking out back, the cold air hits me, sending a chill down my spine. The alley behind the club was completely dark, with only the light of the moon to illuminate the shiny dumpster. After tossing the bag of trash into the dumpster, I headed back to the back door. As I was about to reach for the handle, I felt a presence behind me and in the blink of an eye, my front was pressed to the dirty brick wall. I quickly went into fight mode, trying to push away from the wall to get away from whoever this asshole was. I felt the warm breath of the person on my neck and was overwhelmed with a sweet mahogany scent and scotch.

"What the fuck do you think you're doing, Damon?" I growled between clenched teeth. I could feel the hard planes of his muscular body pressed against my back and everywhere our bodies connected, my skin grew heated.

He slipped his hand into the hair at the nape of my neck, gripping tightly and jerking my head back so that I was forced to look up at him. He had a mischievous smirk on his face that I really just wanted to stab with my knife.

"I just wanted to talk to you. I found some interesting information I thought you might help me with."

I just glared at him as he pressed himself harder against my back. This bastard was playing games I wasn't interested in playing. "What do you want?"

"I want to know why you are really here, Angel. Does it have something to do with my father's connection to Jessica?" He said as he held his face in my hair.

I felt myself hold my breath as my heart rate increased. How had he fucking figured that out? If he knew what I was up to, I was as good as dead. I refused to be taken out before I finished what I had started. I moved my hand down to my knife, ready to fight my way out of this if I had to. Before my hand could wrap around the hilt, his free hand gripped my wrist, and he tsked at me like he was scolding a child.

"That's not very nice, Angel," He slipped his hand lower, removing my knife and dragging the sharp edge up along my thigh, "I was hoping we could help each other."

The sensation of the knife and his breath along my neck was wreaking havoc on my mind. I didn't like the reactions he had on my body. "I don't know what you're talking about." Hissing, I pushed back against him.

I could feel him smile against me as he tossed the knife to the side, replacing it with his rough, callused hands. Goosebumps broke across my skin and my breath hitched slightly.

"Don't play dumb, Angel. You're smarter than that."

He slipped his hand from my thigh to in between my legs, running his fingers along my covered slit. When his fingers pressed firmly to my clit, my body automatically responded by grinding harder into his hand. What the fuck was wrong with me?

He chuckled at my reaction to his ministrations and began working the throbbing bundle of nerves through my shorts. A breathy moan slipped from my lips and my thoughts scattered. I didn't know what power he had over me, but I couldn't stop my reactions. Warnings blared in my ears that I should fight back. He was onto me and I needed to get away from him.

"Tell me the truth Angel, then I'll make you come harder than you ever have in your life." He growled deeply as he continued to pleasure me with his fingers.

Without thinking, the words spilled from my lips, "I want him dead."

"Good girl," He removed his hands from my aching core and spun me to face him, pinning my arms at my sides, "consider it done."

I stared at him in complete shock. I just confessed to wanting to kill his father, and he had agreed. It couldn't be that simple. This had to be some sort of sick game. His hands slipped from my arms, one wrapping around my throat, while the other worked on the buttons of my shorts. He slipped his hand inside and growled as he felt my wet center. My body had a mind of its own where he was concerned.

"So wet for me, Angel." He nearly purred as his fingers slipped inside of me while the palm of his hand worked my clit and I gripped the wrist around my throat. I bit my lip, trying to stifle the moans, wanting to slip past.

He continued to work my center until I could feel my walls gripping his fingers. I was so close already. He moved his hand into my hair as he crashed his mouth to mine. It was a hungry sort of kiss, and he was completely in control. I gripped his broad shoulders to steady myself as I kissed him back, biting and nipping at his lips and tongue. Moaning into his mouth as I came apart on his hand. As soon as the waves of pleasure had passed, he removed his hand from my shorts and slipped back into the club, leaving me breathless, leaning against the wall. What had

just happened?

As soon as I got back to my crappy apartment, I

collapsed onto my bed. The metal frame squeaked loudly in

the small space. I couldn't get the night and everything that

had happened with Damon out of my head. My body was

on fire from his touch.

I had attempted to find him once I had gained my

composure, but Zack said he had already left for the night.

I needed to find out why he had acted the way he did. Why

manipulate me into telling him my goal and then touch me

the way he did? What game was he playing at?

The questions filled my mind as I lay there trying to

get to sleep. I would have to confront him tomorrow if he

was at the club. When it was obvious, I wasn't getting any

sleep. I got up and turned on some crappy TV show to clear my head.

I awoke with a start when there was a knock on my door. Glancing at the time on my phone, seeing it was just past noon. I must have fallen asleep last night while watching TV. Slipping off the couch, I decided it was best to see what was at the door. Doing so, I found a bouquet of red roses on my welcome mat. I looked around to see the hallway empty before picking up the flowers and shutting the door behind me. Walking into my small kitchen area, I sat the roses down, fishing out the card to see who they were from.

I can't wait to see you tonight. -D

I scoffed, rolling my eyes and tossing the card on the counter. I needed to figure out what he was planning so that I could make sure I came out on top.

Deciding it was probably best to shower and get ready for my shift at Hellfire. Taking my time to shower, applying light smokey makeup, and tossing on a pair of ripped jeans along with a black, strappy crop top. Tonight, I would wear my knife in my thigh holster, so that it was easier to get to in case I ended up needing it. I had a feeling death was stalking me at the moment and I wouldn't go down without a fight.

Once I was ready, I decided I was going to take my bike instead of the car today. I admired her before climbing on. It had taken me a while to save up for her, but her smooth riding was well worth it. A blacked-out 2016 Harley-Davidson Breakout. I always loved how freeing it felt to ride her down the winding roads outside of the city.

As soon as all this was over, I planned to hop on my bike and ride to wherever the road took me. As far from my bloody past as possible.

CHAPTER SIX

Damon

Zack was running me through the weekly drink specials he had come up with when I saw Angel walk through the front door. She held a bike helmet under her arm as she made her way over. I didn't take her as the type to be into riding, but the thought of her straddling my bike had my cock straining against my jeans.

I appeared to be listening intently to Zack rather than watching her slip behind the bar. She was in a crop top and ripped jeans today. I had to admit I loved her casual attire and the way her jeans hugged her curvaceous ass.

"Sounds good, Zack," I said in approval before turning my gaze fully toward Angel.

"Hey there, Angel," I smirked her way, dragging my eyes down to her figure.

I noticed a slight dusting of color along her cheeks as she nodded toward me, slipping her helmet into a cabinet under the bar. Zack simply glanced between us like he could feel the tension in the air. He cleared his throat before announcing that he was going to the back to grab some extra bottles. Once he was gone, I got up from my stool at the bar and walked over to where Angel was getting things straightened out before the night began. Was she purposely trying to avoid looking at me? That just wouldn't do.

I approached her from behind and caged her in against the bar with my arms on either side of her. She tensed as her hands paused from where she was whipping the bar in front of her.

"What are you playing at, Damon?" She asked in that sultry voice I loved, just barely above a whisper.

"I believe I made that perfectly clear last night," I breathed against the back of her neck, watching her shiver, "We both want my father dead. I believe we can help each other."

She glanced at me over her shoulder. "And what about the rest?"

I couldn't help the grin that graced my lips. I couldn't get the little sounds she made as she came apart on my hand last night out of my head. She could have stopped me easily, instead she had let me bring her pleasure. I'd be the first to admit I had to fuck my hand three times before I could even think of sleeping. I couldn't stay away from her and I knew that the fact that I affected her was something she wasn't the happiest about. Instead of answering her question, I simply pushed away from the bar and began my way to the office in the back.

She would get answers tonight when Dimitri got the chance to speak with her. Until then, she'd simply have to deal with the unanswered questions. The business side of things was easy. Dimitri would take care of making the plan while I was sure Angel and I would handle the dirty details. It was the draw to her I wasn't sure about. She was a challenge for me, and I wanted to break her in the most pleasurable ways possible. I wanted her to bleed so beautifully for me.

CHAPTER SEVEN

It was another busy night, with Saturday being much busier than the night before. Cherry was helping Zack behind the bar while I was maintaining orders for the floor and VIP areas. We worked our asses off serving drinks and appetizers through the night and I couldn't help the sigh of relief once we had closed up. Damon had even disappeared after that first encounter of the evening.

I sat down at the bar, downing a glass of water while Zack was finishing up inventory for the night. "So, where did Cherry disappear to?"

"She slipped upstairs to see Dimitri." Zack said, throwing a wink over his shoulder.

I was surprised. From what I had seen of Dimitri, he was the calm businessman type, whereas Cherry was bubbly and a ray of sunshine. It may have made sense if the whole 'opposites attract' thing was something to be believed.

We had finished everything up for closing by the time Cherry made her way back to us. She skipped her way over to the bar and took a seat next to me.

"The boys want to see you back in the office?" She said with a sweet smile and a wink.

"Uh oh, sounds like someone is in trouble." Zack taunted with a grin as he ate his hundredth bowl of peanuts of the night. The boy had a strange addiction to the damn things.

I just rolled my eyes at both of them and made my way toward the back office. Once I made it to the door, I rapped my knuckles on the red oak door a few times.

"Come in, Angel." I heard Damon growl from the other side of the door. The tenor of his voice sent shivers down my spine.

I opened the door and walked in to find Dimitri sitting behind the desk, running his hands through his dark hair. He looked like the weight of the world rested on his shoulders and had a permanent scowl on his face. It was still so hard to imagine him and the bubbly Cherry together. Damon was leaning against the edge of the desk with a cigarette held between his teeth as he flashed me a crooked smirk. I quickly glanced away from him and focused on Dimitri.

"Let's get this over with, shall we?" I spoke with more confidence than I felt as I took a seat in front of them. To keep my hands busy, I took out my knife and began cleaning my nails with it.

Dimitri was the first to speak up, folding his hands in front of himself on the desk. "I need to know everything. What you have planned, why you're after our father, everything, Ms. Hart."

I took the chance to glance at Damon from the corner of my eye before focusing back on Dimitri, laying my knife on the desk in front of me. "Your father's responsible for the rape and murder of my younger sister. I planned on getting close to him and killing him. It's as simple as that."

"And is that why you killed all those other men, Angel?" Damon spoke as he put out his cigarette in a nearby ashtray.

"Yes," was my simple answer. I wasn't showing these guys any fear. I wasn't scared of them. If they had wanted me dead, they would have done it by now. Made it look like an accident.

"I want to know the details of those other deaths." Dimitri said, grabbing my attention again.

I recounted the death of every man I had killed so far. Explaining how I'd used my body to my advantage and took them out as soon as I got any needed information out of them. I explained what had happened to Jessica and how her "boyfriend" had been the first man I had killed in order to find out all the names of those involved in her murder. I even went as far as showing them the footage I'd saved from our security system. They didn't even make it a few minutes into the video before cutting it off and handing the phone back. The shit was sick, so I completely understood their reaction.

It was odd telling these two all the gory details of my life following the day I walked in to find my sister's mutilated body. It felt freeing to finally talk to someone about it. I had no family, no friends, and had been utterly alone for the past eight years. It was as if a weight had been lifted from me, but I still had to remain cautious. I couldn't exactly trust these two.

It became clear who the man in charge was, so I focused all my attention on Dimitri. He was going to be the one who determined my fate. "What reason would you have to talk to me rather than kill me? Madax is your father, regardless of what he's done, and he's essentially your boss."

"We want the old fuck dead as much as you do, Angel," Damon said as he plopped down in a chair next to me.

I kept quiet, waiting for him or Dimitri to elaborate, "He's destroying the business slowly and we've lost credibility with many of our former partners. Not everyone in the underground is interested in working with human trafficking. They are pulling their funds and siding with our competitors. We have been biding our time, waiting for the best moment to take him out so that we can take over the business." Dimitri said as he watched me closely.

"And what does this have to do with me?"

"We want you to be the one to end him. Essentially, you get your revenge and we keep our hands clean. We will help you as needed to get close to him. However, I have some things to work out before he can be eliminated." Dimitri leveled me with a glare before standing up to pour himself a glass of scotch across the room.

"What you mean is that if I am caught, I go down," I state, glancing between the two brothers.

Damon just grinned as he eyed me, and Dimitri pretended like I was simply an inconvenience. I got the feeling he didn't like or trust me very much. Good, at least he wasn't stupid.

"Okay, I'm in. Now, how do you intend to get me close to Madax?" I asked.

CHAPTER EIGHT

After agreeing to work with us, Dimitri explained how

Angel could get close to our shit bag father. He instructed

her to take Cherry's place serving in the VIP lounge, where

my father planned to have a meeting. We'd spent the entire

week preparing her, though I knew she'd do things her own

way. She was a fucking minx who didn't take orders well.

Once her mind was made up, she wouldn't stop until she

got what she wanted. I couldn't wait to see her in action

tonight.

    I watched her as she worked the crowd. She'd

decided on a short skirt and crop top for tonight as she

served and took orders down below on the main floor.

Those thigh-high boots made her long legs even more

delectable. I wasn't happy that she planned to seduce my father. I wanted her attention on me, but I knew I couldn't let my possessiveness get in the way. This plan had to work. My father and his business partners would arrive soon and I'd get to see her in action, but I wanted her to myself before their arrival. I made a call down to the bar, asking Zack to send her up with some drinks to start the night.

I continued to watch her as she worked before making her way to the bar. She was speaking to Zack and handed her orders off to Cherry before glancing up at the window to the lounge. Even though I knew she couldn't see me, it was as if she was staring right at me. I felt my cock hardening against my slacks as I watched her make her way upstairs with a tray of bottles and empty glasses.

When she walked into the room, I had already taken a seat on a sofa as she began setting everything out on the private bar. She was so much fun to watch as she made a glass of scotch before making her way over to me. The way she walked was sensual, with little effort on her part. She bent down to place the tumbler on the glass table in front of me, and I couldn't help but to slide my hand up her thigh to her luscious ass. It was round and fit perfectly in my hands. Hooking my other hand around the opposite thigh, I pulled her towards me, forcing her to straddle my lap. She was tense, but I could see the hunger in those cold eyes of hers.

"What do you want, Damon?" She sounded absolutely bored. I wasn't sure if she was trying to convince me or herself at this point that she didn't want me.

"I just wanted to see what you had on underneath this little skirt of yours," I said as I slipped my finger underneath her lacy thong, running my fingers lightly along her slit until I was at her wet, hot center.

I inserted a finger, fucking her slowly as her breath caught. "So wet for me, Angel."

"I'm just excited about tonight." She gasped as she gripped tighter onto my shoulders.

I smirked, adding a second figure into her wet cunt. "So the idea of killing a man makes you this wet?"

Her only response was a breathy moan as I curved my fingers to rub that sensitive little spot inside of her. She ground her hips, trying to get more friction where she needed it. This was going to be a fun little game of getting her to admit that she wanted me. My Angel was stubborn.

I quickly flipped her over onto the couch, pinning her down with my free hand as I kissed my way down her throat. She pushed against me as if her fight was restored, which just made me pin her down harder. Removing my fingers from her dripping wet cunt, I gripped the crotch of her thong, ripping the flimsy fabric from her body. She gasped, pausing in her fight to get away from me as she watched me wide-eyed. I tucked the torn panties into my back pocket before kissing my way down her body as my fingers worked her clit.

"Be a good girl for me, Angel, and I'll let you come." I whispered against her breast as I took her nipple into my mouth through her shirt.

"Fuck you," she moaned, using her hips to wiggle her way from underneath me.

I bit her nipple harder, forcing a pained noise to escape her throat. "Play nice."

I wanted both her pain and pleasure. I planned to take her whether she wanted it or not at that moment. Her powerless fight did nothing but make me harder for her. I licked down her exposed stomach, delighting in the shivers my tongue invoked. She continued to worm her way out of my grip as my mouth reached its destination between her soft thighs. I wasted no time devouring her, moving my hands to pin her legs open. Her sweet taste exploded on my tongue and I ate her like a starved man. She slipped her hand into my hair, pulling on the lengths hard as my name slipped from her full lips. I'm not sure if she intended to pull me off or force me to stay, but it would take more than her to stop me from feasting on her. I bit and sucked until she was grinding her pussy against my face, mewling like the little demon she was as I took from her. If I was ever to die, I wanted her cunt to be my last meal on this earth. Slipping my fingers into her and focusing my mouth on her swollen clit, I worked her into a frenzy. Oh, so quickly her walls clamped around my fingers as her orgasm overtook her. Her screams of pleasure filled the room as I feasted on her. Before she could come down, I unbuttoned my slacks, freeing my rock-hard cock. I quickly slipped up her body and slammed into her, as her pussy gripped my length. A moan slipped from my lips at just the feeling of her warm heat wrapped around my shaft. She tried to claw at my face to fight me off, so I pinned her hands above her head as I pistoned into her hard and fast.

"Get the fuck off me," she screamed, bucking her hips, which only forced me deeper inside of her wet center.

I grinned, leaning my face down to hers, "Now, why would I do that when you're taking me so well, Angel?"

Before she could scream at me, I captured her mouth with mine in a hungry and angry kiss. There was nothing nice about it with her teeth biting my lip until I could taste blood. The metallic taste sent me into a frenzy and I wanted to make her bleed just as badly. I fucked her harder as I slipped my knife from my pocket with my free hand. The blade traveled up her thigh as I slowed my thrusts. At the feeling of the blade, she stopped fighting me and I leaned up to watch her as I slipped the blade to the inside of her thigh next to where I was fucking her.

"I asked you to play nice, Angel."

My response was simply a glare as I smiled down at her. She was at my mercy and she knew it. I stalled my thrust as I dug the tip of my blade into her skin. The blood seeped from the minor wound in the most beautiful shade of red. A hiss left her lips as I continued to slice a D into her delicate flesh. Once I was satisfied, I slipped out of her, released her hands, and leaned down to lick away the blood. I groaned at the metallic flavor mixed in with her unique taste. She had become my new favorite dessert.

"You will always belong to me, Angel." I glanced up at her to see her reaction. If looks could kill, I'd be a dead man.

"I belong to no man." She spat, though the fight seemed to have completely left her.

"Keep telling yourself that, baby girl." I sat back on the couch and pulled her so that she was on top of me, forcing her hands behind her back. Quickly sheathing myself back into her wet cunt, and thrust my hips up. I wanted to break her. I wanted to have her begging for my cock, but I enjoyed every moment of her fight until she was coming on my dick.

CHAPTER NINE

Angel

The first to arrive, only a few minutes after Damon had released me, was Dimitri who shot a glare at his brother, after he had caught me trying to get myself together and Damon tucking himself back into his slacks. I felt my face heat as he eyed us both.

"I see you two are getting to know each other better." He sighed, going over and pouring himself a glass of scotch.

Damon simply chuckled deeply as he took a swing from his tumbler, eyeing me over the rim of the glass. He was so openly proud of himself while I was trying to get over the confusion. My body wasn't getting the memo that I wasn't interested, much like Damon didn't know how to take no for an answer. Yet, the feeling of his come leaking down the inside of my thighs and the burn where he'd cut me had me wanting to do it all over again.

I went over and finished stocking the small private bar, making sure that I had everything I would need for the evening. I had every intention of pretending like Damon didn't exist and that what happened was a one-time thing. It was simply to get it out of my system so I could focus on my mission. He wanted to own me and he was shit out of luck if he thought he ever had a chance.

A group of businessmen in three-piece suits arrived shortly after Dimitri, followed by the one and only Madax. He entered the room and my blood ran cold. I felt suffocated, like his presence sucked up every bit of air in this small room. I forced myself to take a deep breath, plastered a sweet smile on my face as I greeted each man entering the room, and took their orders for the evening.

As I made everyone's drinks I watched Madax from the corner of my eye. He was fairly attractive for a man in his early sixties. He had short cut salt and pepper hair that he wore slicked back and a well-groomed matching beard. His chocolate eyes watched me closely as he spoke with the other businessmen. I could tell he was muscular and toned underneath his suit with just a hint of tattoos peeking out here and there. It was obvious where Damon and Dimitri got their tall, built frames. They each carried a sense of confidence about themselves and took pride in their appearance.

Dimitri was the most businesslike and conservative of the three. He had the same light brown hair as Damon, but was clean-shaven, had no noticeable tattoos, and carried himself like I would imagine a politician. He was calm and collected, watching everything going on with poise, and if you weren't paying enough attention, you'd miss the tick in his jaw and flex of his fingers around his glass every time someone said something he didn't like.

Madax carried himself in the same fashion as Dimitri and was presented as a businessman. The only difference was that the tattoos gave him a slightly rough around the edges look. That he could play the part of a gentleman, but he's also put a bullet in your head if you crossed him.

Damon was the most brutal of the bunch. You could tell he took pride in his appearance like the other two, but he was laid back in his dress and demeanor. He was the kinda bad boy the ladies would trip over to get just a second of his time. His smirk that lifted just noticeably higher on the left side, and the excited twinkle in his eye made him dangerous. He was a wolf in sheep's clothing that would take pleasure in killing a man.

These men were each dangerous in their own way.

Loading my tray up with the drinks and making my way around the room, saving Madax for last. I smiled at him while he watched me like a predator who had just spotted its next kill. I leaned down to hand him his glass, and he quickly placed his hand on my thigh.

"You're the new girl, darling?" He drawled in his seductive tenor. I bet that worked on all the young girls. All I wanted to do was break the fingers that were trailing lightly up my leg.

I decided playing shy would be the best route to go, so I forced myself to blush. "Yes, sir."

I was a perfect fucking actress. I'd been playing this role for the past eight years and the men I set my sights on always ate out of the palm of my hands.

He smirked as he slid his hand to the back of my knee and pulled me closer. "Why don't you sit next to me for now and relax? We are all good with drinks for the time being."

It wasn't a request, and I knew it. Stealing a glance at Damon, who was watching the exchange from across the coffee table. Anger filled his eyes and his grip on the tumbler in his hand had tightened enough to leave him white-knuckled. I sat next to Madax while his hand rested just above my knee as he went back to talking business with the other men. I didn't care to learn their names or even understand most of what they spoke of. Cattle, stock, livestock, and market were mentioned, but from the sounds of things, I had the sinking feeling they weren't talking about farm animals. I sat perfectly still, unable to fully relax while watching the interactions between them. As the night drew on, Madax's hand would work its way up my thigh and he'd try to include me in the conversations. While I wasn't comfortable, Madax was as gentlemanly as a snake of his kind could be. I guess that was part of the allure. He may be the gentleman on the outside, but I knew he was far from a good man. My sister's dead body proved that.

"Angel, would you mind grabbing me another?" Damon asked, shaking his empty glass. I nearly jumped at the opportunity.

"Of course, sir," I said as I made my way over to retrieve his empty glass. He grabbed my wrist lightly as he whispered so that only I could hear.

"You're doing great. Just try not to kill him yet." He smirked.

I shot him a glare, "I'm aware," I growled under my breath as I took his glass and went to get him and the others a refill.

Thankfully, Madax didn't pay me much mind while he finished conducting business. I went about cleaning up from the evening and doing an inventory of everything that would need to be restocked for the private bar.

I didn't turn around to face the men as they each filed out of the room, so it came as a surprise when a hand rested on my lower back and the smell of gin fanned across the side of my face.

"Thank you for the service tonight, darling." Madax breathed across my neck. His hand skating lower on my ass. Not enough to make him out as a complete pervert, but enough to get the message that he was interested.

"It was my pleasure, sir."

He placed a gentle kiss on my cheek, slipped a crisp $100 bill on my tray, and walked towards the door. I stood there with my hands clenched at my sides until I heard the click of the door shutting. Without thinking, I grabbed a tumbler and hurled it at the wall, watching as it shattered.

He'd been right fucking there, with his hands on me most of the night, and I'd had to play nice instead of killing him and all those posh business men.

Damon chuckled behind me, and I glared at him over my shoulder. "What's so fucking funny?"

He walked over to me, lightly running his fingertips up my arm, "The fact that you're such a good little actress. You nearly had me convinced with the shy, innocent act," he slid his fingers up my shoulder before wrapping his hand around my neck, forcing me onto my tiptoes to be in his face, "I know much better than that, Angel."

He caged me up to the bar top as he spoke lightly, running his fingers along my arms as he placed gentle kisses along my neck.

"What happened tonight won't be happening again." I shrugged him off to go clean up the glass all over the floor.

"Keep telling yourself that, Angel." He walked out without glancing my way, leaving me to clean up my mess.

CHAPTER TEN

Angel

The rest of the weekend and the beginning of the week went as normal following the meeting with Madax. He hadn't shown up again at the club after his business partners left Saturday night. After the meeting, I had to rush home and scrub my skin to the point of pain before I felt clean. That was the biggest downfall of doing crap like this. I felt dirty until I could wash that grim away with the blood of the men who'd hurt Jessica.

It was Thursday afternoon at the club when I received any contact from Madax. I received a delivery, which included a diamond Tiffany necklace and a note saying, *I haven't been able to stop thinking about you.* What was the deal with the Ashford men thinking they could just touch me and send me gifts afterward, like it was completely normal? The thought alone made me roll my eyes and toss the jewelry box into the cabinet that housed my belongings during work hours.

Things had been weird between Damon and me since our short fling. He'd kept his distance, only lightly brushing me in passing, and I would constantly feel his eyes on me whenever he was at Hellfire during my shifts. I wasn't sure about my feelings anymore and the on-and-off-again thing was really pissing me off, no matter how hard I tried to ignore the entire situation. I finished my shift and headed straight home to collapse on my bed. The events of the past week had exhausted my system, but I needed to get my shit together. I could worry about all that tomorrow.

I awoke to a knock on my door and pulled my blankets high above my head. It was far too early for people to be knocking on my door on a Friday morning. My head was pounding, and I felt like I hadn't slept nearly enough. After waiting a good 15 minutes, I got up to see what those Ashfords had sent this time.

Opening the door, there was a decently sized white box tied with a cream-colored silk ribbon. Picking it up, I closed the door and fished out the little card.

Be ready in this by 5pm. I will have a car sent to pick you up. Don't worry about work, I have cleared it with your boss. -Madax

Opening the box, I found a white dress and a matching lace mask. Glancing at the clock, it was almost three in the afternoon. I'd slept longer than I had realized, yet was still feeling run down. Since it was going to be a formal event, I might as well get ready. I bathed, taking extra care of my beauty routine, before getting dressed. Slipping into the dress, it fell to the floor to pool out around my feet. It was a floor-length white gown with slits up both sides to my hips, with a tulle-covered skirt that did little to cover up the exposed skin. It had spaghetti straps and a deep plunging neckline that fell to my navel. I took time to apply light, natural makeup with my usual bold red lip. Something about the color gave me a sense of power and control when dealing with the men I'd been hunting. I threw my hair up in a messy yet elegant, low bun, leaving stray pieces to frame my face in natural waves. To finish the look, I slipped on a pair of gold gladiator heels and the white lace masquerade mask. Looking at myself in the mirror, I barely recognized myself. I looked elegant and sophisticated. Worst of all, the white color of this dress made me sick. Why couldn't it have been something

darker?

At exactly 5pm there was a knock on the door and

I took one more chance to make sure everything was

perfect. I opened the door to see who my escort would be

for the evening. My breath caught in my throat seeing

Damon standing there in an all-black tux, shiny black

loafers, and his long hair tied up into a sleek high bun. He'd

taken the time to groom his roguish beard, and I had the

sudden urge to touch it. It had surprised me at how soft it

felt when he went down on me Saturday night. His blue

eyes traveled over my body like a heated caress, and I felt

my face flush. He smirked in the charming, crooked way

that only he could when his eyes met mine again and he

stepped to the side, offering me his arm.

Glaring at him, I slipped my arm into his as he

escorted me out of the building. We definitely didn't seem

to fit into my crappy apartment building dressed like this. I'd never felt so out of place here. Damon didn't seem to pay it any mind as he led me out front to an elegant black limo. He opened the door, allowing me to slide in before he took a seat next to me.

"I wasn't expecting you to pick me up when I got the letter from Madax." I glanced anywhere but at him.

He slid his hand up my neck before forcing me to look at him. "I wouldn't miss a chance to have you to myself."

His voice was deep as he gripped my chin, pulling me closer to him. His free hand inched up my exposed thigh until he reached my center, a groan leaving his lips when he noticed that there was nothing underneath my dress.

"Angel," He growled, claiming my lips with his.

The kiss was hungry and forceful. I kissed him back just as furiously. My hands gripped the front of his jacket as I worked the buttons loose in a frenzy to get to him. He pushed me back onto the seat while he sat between my legs, lifting the skirt of my dress up, baring my aching center to him and his mercy. So much for not letting this happen again.

He leaned down to trail kisses up my thighs as he reached behind him, pulling a hidden handgun out, which he laid on the seat next to him. At the sight of it, I gasped, sitting up and sliding away from him. My retreat must have been amusing, because he just smirked at me, a dark chuckle leaving him as his hand wrapped around my ankle to keep me from moving too far.

"Don't worry, baby girl. That isn't for hurting you." He cornered me, pinning me to the side of the limo by my throat, and slid his finger up my inner thigh.

He took his time exploring the valleys between my thighs with his free hand, sending goosebumps down my legs. His sinful mouth trailed kisses along my chest and the hand around my throat moved to release my cleavage from the dress. He took my peaked nipple into his mouth, biting down on the tinder flesh to the point of pain. It was a direct line to my wet center, and I tried to grind my hip to get any sort of friction where I needed it. He chuckled, causing his beard to tickle me where I was most sensitive, and he moved his teasing hand to my swollen clit.

"Is this what you want, Angel?" He asked before taking my other nipple into his mouth.

"Fuck… yes." I moaned out breathlessly.

This man knew exactly what he was doing. He slipped two fingers into my pussy while his thumb worked my clit. My nails dug into his shoulders as I rode his hand, seeking the pleasure my body craved. He moved down my body in a fluid motion until he was between my legs, moving his hand to take my clit into his mouth. Sucking and biting to give me the perfect mix of pain and pleasure. I'd never thought of myself as a masochist, but every time he hurt me, it turned me on.

As he worked me with his fingers and expert tongue, I watched as he reached for the gun he'd taken out earlier. The cold metal of the gun trailed my thigh to my wet center, sending shivers in its wake. Damon forced my legs wider, replacing his fingers with the gun, as he ran his tongue along my slit. The sensation of his rough beard, his warm tongue, and the cold of the gun sliding along my center had me panting. I felt him smile against my skin as he slowly pushed the barrel into me, forcing a breathy moan to escape my lips.

"You're taking it so well, Angel. Has anyone ever made you come like this?" He asked, lifting his head to look at me. I couldn't seem to form words as I shook my head. He began thrusting the gun into me at a hard yet leisurely pace. The cold and unusual feeling forced me to moan in pleasure. He had the gun angled just right to stimulate that sweet spot within me, and his hand rubbed my clit for the perfect amount of friction.

"That's it, baby girl. I want to watch you come on my gun." He purred as he thrust it harder and faster. My pussy clenched tightly around the barrel as he brought me closer to my release.

Damon lowered his mouth back between my legs and I felt as he licked the healing mark where he'd brand me. How could the fact that he'd marked me in such a way make me feel cherished and so fucking turned on at the same time? I rocked my hips, moaning out his name softly.

"Fuck… Damon… please don't stop."

"I love it when you beg." He groaned before moving his mouth to my center, taking my clit into his mouth, sucking and biting at it in the perfect rhythm to match the thrusts of his gun.

I gripped his hair tightly as I rode his mouth and gun. All I could focus on was the pleasure he was bringing me as I screamed out my release. The feeling of my pussy clenching around the gun's barrel had me tipping over the edge harder than I ever had. He devoured me like his favorite meal through the waves of pleasure until I was gasping to catch my breath.

He removed the gun from between my legs, lifting it to my lips. "Clean up your mess, baby girl."

I wrapped my lips around the barrel, moaning at the flavor of myself mixed with the metallic taste of the gun. I never took my eyes off his as I cleaned my release from his gun, removing it from my mouth with an audible pop.

He slipped the gun back into its holster on the waistband of his pants and helped me into a seated position, pulling me closer to his side, and peppered light kisses along my neck, whispering praises.

"Such a good girl, Angel." He placed one more rough kiss against my lips before pulling my dress back into place to cover me. "We will be there in just a moment."

I was still completely at a loss for words. I wasn't sure why I let him touch me when I'd already said it wouldn't happen again. Lost in thought, I glanced out the window and watched as we pulled through the iron gates of a large estate. The driveway was paved and lined with beautiful trees that were changing colors in the growing autumn atmosphere. It led up to a large white colonial estate that screamed money. Everything was lit up and appeared to glow in the dusk that was descending over the horizon. In another life, I may have found it beautiful, but I had learned that most beautiful things were a mask meant to hide someone's dirty secrets.

As we pulled to a stop, I watched as others dressed in flowing gowns and tuxedos made their way through the elegant double-doors of the estate. The women appeared to be the only ones wearing masks for this event. Damon climbed out first, offering me his hand as he helped me to stand. I made sure that my dress was in place after our little adventure on the way here, before Damon led me up the front steps. Everything with the house was almost comical, with its white and gold accents, oversized double doors, white marbled floors, expensive artwork, crystal chandeliers, and the grand double staircase that was the centerpiece as you entered the foyer.

Damon led us to an extravagant, golden ballroom that was filled with people for whatever this occasion was. I took in every exit I could use if needed and watched as servers offered champagne and hors d'oeuvres to the guests. We made our way to the back corner of the room where I could see Madax surrounded by a group that was hanging on to his every word, as he spoke of how his family came into power and made their first billion. I scoffed under my breath, which just made Damon smile.

"Play nice tonight, Angel." He said, patting my hand lightly.

As we neared, Madax's eyes snagged on me. Eyeing me like the predator he was as he took in every inch of my exposed skin. I felt my hand tighten on Damon's arm and he squeezed it in reassurance before presenting me to Madax.

"Sir," He said, moving my hand from his arm to place into his father's.

"Thank you for escorting this lovely woman for me this evening, son." Madax pulled me close to him, wrapping an arm around my waist and resting his hand far too low on my hips for me to be comfortable. I simply smiled up at him. These Ashford men had a way of making a girl feel small with their 6 feet plus of stature. I wasn't short, standing at 5'5", but they made me feel small. Damon was slightly taller than his father by a few inches, as he stood off to the other side of Madax, speaking to an elderly man in the group.

Pressed into his side, Madax went on with his previous conversation while I pretended to hang onto his every word, like the others in our small circle. Glancing away from Madax, I noticed that Damon had slipped away.

I could just barely see him standing at the bar along the wall closest to our little group through the growing crowd.

He kept watch like this throughout the night as Madax paraded us around the room and light instrumentals played. It became clear quickly that I was to be seen and not heard. So I played the part of the dutiful mistress, who smiled and nodded when appropriate. Only speaking when directly spoken to, as I noticed the other women doing. As I walked around the room, I also noticed the sheer lack of women. What was the point of so few women and why were we the only ones wearing masks?

I watched as Madax waved Damon back over towards us and he said goodbye to the group he was finishing up speaking to. When Damon got closer, he offered me his arm, and I was thankful as Madax let me go to him.

"Damon, keep Angel company while I finish business for the evening," He ordered before turning his attention to me, "Darling, please stay close to my son for the rest of the evening. I promise you will have my full attention once I'm finished with tonight's event."

I smiled at him as he kissed my hand lightly before making his way through the crowd to the large stage set off to the far side of the room. Damon placed his hand on the small of my back as he led me as far from the stage as he could. Dimitri was standing next to the door that led back out to the front of the house, and I waved slightly as he cut a glare in my direction. Him not liking me brought a smile to my face. He was right not to trust me. I'd proven that I was a wildcard in their plan, but we needed each other's help.

We stood against the wall together, with me between the two Ashford brothers, as the room fell into darkness and a spotlight shone towards the stage where Madax stood behind a white podium. It was obvious he really liked the color white.

Damon leaned down, placing his lips against the shell of my ear, forcing a shiver to work down my spine. "This next part of the night you aren't going to like."

I glanced up at him to meet his eyes as he straightened, tilting his head towards the stage and pulled me in closer to his side. The room had fallen silent as Madax became the center of attention.

"Thank you, everyone, for joining me this evening. We have a large stock tonight and I'm sure you will all be very pleased. Tonight's stock is full of fresh, untouched products," Madax smiled at the crowd as a line of women were brought onto the stage. They were each in chains and dressed in all colors of lingerie.

The crowd cheered and clapped while I just stood there frozen. My breath caught in my throat as I gaped at the stage. I was sure my face looked like those old cartoons where their jaws hit the floor. I had been expecting bad things from Madax, but this was an auction for women and girls to be sold off like property. Every muscle in my body tensed and I saw red as the first girl, probably no older than 16, was auctioned off to the highest bidder. I couldn't tear my eyes from each girl with tear-streaked faces being sold off like cattle. Never had I felt a blood lust so apparent that I could taste it. I had wanted him dead before. Now I wanted to watch him bleed out in front of me. I want to hurt him, not only for my sister, but for every girl that has ever stood on that stage.

What sort of sick fuck could do this to other people? I went to pull away from Damon, but he just held me tighter, pinning me to his side as he watched the scene play out in front of us. Glancing at his face, I could see the same anger in his eyes that I was feeling. He wasn't on board with this bullshit which made me like him more.

"We don't like this any more than you do." I heard Dimitri's gruff voice on my other side.

"He's a dead man walking," Damon growled as he ground his teeth.

Glancing around, we were the only three in this room that didn't like what we were seeing. I silently wondered if the other women here were upset by what was going on or if they just simply supported it. They just stood there and partook in this shit and I wanted to hurt them, too. How could they just stand there and allow it?

We simply stood there in silent, boiling anger as each girl was sold and escorted away to be claimed at the end of the night. I don't know how I simply stood and watched. Every fiber of my being was begging to be let loose on this crowd of monsters. I might not be a saint, but I wasn't downright evil. Not like this. Damon's arm stayed locked around my waist, holding me in place as the night went on. Twenty-three girls were sold that night, ranging from the age of 16 to 25.

As they sold the last girl, a toast was made, and the crowd filled out. Either to leave for the evening or to collect their prize. Dimitri slipped off and Damon led me upstairs away from the people, into what he said was a guest room I'd be using during my stay here.

By this point, I was in a daze as I sank down onto the edge of the bed and simply stared at the bare, white walls of the room. Damon crouched down in front of me, taking my hands in his and placed soft kisses along my knuckles.

"This is part of the reason that we wanted your help. He expects Dimitri and I to try something. You're the only one who can get close to him without raising suspension." He whispered.

I let my eyes roam over his face, looking for any sign that he was lying, only to find none. All I could see was his godly beauty, like some viking warrior kneeling at my feet. I never would have thought I'd find a man as rugged as him, beautiful, but he was. He was a good man who liked to do bad things, and it drew me to him like a moth to a flame. His full lips, soft beard, deep blue eyes that could do in any woman, and in that moment I wanted him. I wanted him to make me forget what I had just witnessed. Without a second thought, I crushed my lips to his, pulling him closer toward me by the collar of his jacket, forcing him in between my legs as I begged him with my mouth to make everything else disappear. Just for a moment. Fuck what I had said. I wasn't sure there would ever be a last time with this man.

He kissed me back, slipping his hand into my hair to angel me just how he wanted me as he ravished me. His tongue demanded entry as he tasted all of me, with a hunger I could only describe as pure Damon. We stayed like that, gripping onto each other, our hands roaming, until someone cleared their throat at the door.

We both startled apart and glanced towards the door, where Madax stood with a glare towards his son. His tuxedo jacket was unbuttoned and his tie undone as he walked into the room running a hand through his slicked back hair. His eyes traveled between me and Madax. I wasn't sure what he saw on my face, but whatever he saw made him smile wickedly.

"I see you two get along fairly well." He said as he slipped off his jacket and tossed it on the bed, rolling up the sleeves of his white dress shirt.

"Let's see just how well." He said as he slid a glare back towards Damon.

CHAPTER ELEVEN

Damon

I simply stood there and watched as my father looked at the two of us. I hadn't meant for us to get caught, and I wasn't sure what the twisted fuck had in mind. Whatever it was, I knew for a fact it was going to piss me off and go too far with Angel. Angel simply watched every move he made with a mix of hate and confusion gleaming in her eyes. Just waiting to see what the old fuck would do next. The smile he was wearing made it obvious he didn't see what I saw on her face.

"Stand up darling, and undress for me." My father instructed her.

She glanced towards me, which only made my father's smile widen. "Oh, he gets to watch, darling."

She looked back at him and stood, slipping the dress off her shoulders for it to pull at her feet, leaving her in nothing but the golden heels she'd worn tonight. Just seeing her bare was making me grow hard and tented my pants. I took a glance at my father to see him adjusting himself as he prowled towards her, running his fingers lightly over her stomach and breast. He whispered praises as he explored her body, slipping his fingers between her legs as he stood behind her, plunging them into her with no warning. He wanted me to watch as he touched her and was making sure I could see everything he did. She simply stood there with a blank look on her beautiful face and her jaw tensed. He continued to finger her as he forced her to lean over the bed with her ass in the air and he continued to work the cunt that belonged to me. Throughout it all, she stayed quiet, breathing through her nose, her body tense. She didn't make the same noises for him as she did for me. That only filled me with pride. I would be the only man to make her feel like that again. I intended to keep my Angel.

It took everything in me to stand there and watch when he unbuttoned his pants to free his lack-luster dick and lined it up with her cunt. The only sound that left her as he thrust into her was a pained gasp and she fisted the sheets, turning her face to look at me as he pounded into her from behind. I couldn't take my eyes off hers. Watching the pain and hatred wash over her features. From the sounds of it, she wasn't wet for him at all as he pounded away at what was mine. No deliciously wet sounds of skin meeting skin that filled the space when I was balls deep in her glorious pussy. The old fuck didn't care if she wanted it or not. He simply demanded it.

"Get on the bed and fuck this whore's face," my father grunted as he continued to fuck her.

I kept watching Angel's face as I made my way over to the bed and climbed in front of her. I undid my pants, freeing my cock as I pulled her up to take me into her mouth. God, her mouth felt so good as I slid between her wet lips. Those blood-red lips wrapped beautifully around my cock. I wanted to fuck up her pretty makeup and have it smeared across her face. The anger in her eyes quickly morphed into hunger as I fucked her mouth roughly, forcing myself deep into her throat. She moaned around my cock, sucking on me. The old fuck might have thought the sounds were for him, but I knew her pleasure was only for me. I wanted this to end for her quickly, but I also wanted to enjoy the filling of her mouth around my straining cock. So, I fucked her mouth just like I would her cunt. Hard and deep. Forcing her to gag on my size as I chased my release. Her saliva dripped down my balls as she took me like a good little slut. Tears ran down her face, leaving blackened streaks down her cheeks. Thank god she could take my size. Few women could.

My father groaned as he pulled out of her, coming over her cunt and ass. He was a fucking idiot if he thought she was his. I stilled my hips without getting my release, pulling out of her mouth to give her some relief. She stayed there panting to catch her breath and cast her eyes down to the now wrinkled duvet.

"Clean her up," my father ordered as he picked up his jacket and left the room without so much as a word towards Angel.

Once he was gone, I quickly cleaned up his mess with my shirt before pulling Angel up into my arms on the bed and forced her onto her back as I crushed my lips to hers. I wanted to brand myself on her. Force every touch my father had inflicted away so that she only remembered mine. That it was only me who her body would sing for.

She kissed me back, clawing at me like a feral feline as her figures tore through my skin. I forced myself between her thighs and slammed my cock deep inside of her wet, warm cunt. Her back arching off the bed from the force as I fucked her hard, just like I knew she liked. Her hands slid around to my back, digging her nails into the skin as she gripped for purchase. I reached between us, finding her clit, rubbing her to create the friction she needed. Oh so quickly, she came apart underneath me with my name falling from her lips. I followed her just as quickly, burying myself deep inside of her as I filled her, her tight cunt milking me through both our releases.

CHAPTER TWELVE

I awoke surrounded by the scent of mahogany and sweet apples. Strong, tattooed arms held me around the waist with my back pressed against a hard chest. Damon had spent the night fucking me until I couldn't remember my name. I didn't even remember falling asleep next to him.

It had been a nice way to end my horrific evening. Between the auction and the feeling of Madax inside of me, I needed a moment to forget. Damon was a wonderful distraction that I was becoming more and more addicted to. The manly scent of him alone had heat pooling in the pit of my stomach and I rubbed my thighs together, moaning at the slight pain it caused. Every ache was caused by Damon's massive cock, and I loved every second of it.

Damon's arm tightened around me, pulling me closer to him as I felt him grind his hard cock between my legs. It rubbed just right against my clit every time, forcing breathy moans to leave my lips. He was already slick from me as he continued to slide along my slit.

"Is this for me, Angel?" He asked. His voice sounded deeper and scratchier with sleep as he woke.

I didn't answer him, instead choosing to enjoy the feeling of him teasing me in the most perfect way. Without any warning, he angled his hips and slammed deep inside of me. He fucked me mercilessly and spent the rest of the morning making me beg for release. It was the sweetest of tortures as he toyed with me, but refused to let me come.

"Don't you dare come, baby girl." He rammed into me with each word.

I was so fucking close and every time he'd get me to that edge he'd order me not to come, "Fuck, please."

I was to the point of begging. Wanting to chase my release, and nearly screamed when his thrusts slowed. I didn't like this game. I didn't like begging him. I'd never begged for anything from a man, and he had accomplished it with hardly any effort.

His thrusts were slow and deliberate as he fucked me from behind, pinning my hands behind my back with only one hand. His other hand smacked my ass as I tried to push my way back to get the friction I'd need to come. "Bad girls don't get to come, Angel."

He slammed into me one last time, sheathing himself to the hilt and held himself there. His hand moved from my seared cheek and traced lightly to my ass, where he pressed his finger in just enough to let me know he was there. A gasp left my lips, and he pushed his finger in just a little deeper. I was so turned on he didn't even need lube.

"Has anyone ever touched you here, Angel?" He asked as he fucked my ass with his finger.

Words failed me and I shook my head, whimpering at the pain and stretch as he added a second finger.

"So tight for me, Angel. I want this ass to be mine, and only mine." He pulled out of me as he continued to fuck my ass and released my hands.

I gripped the sheets as the pain morphed into an aching pleasure. Thrusting my hips back into his hand, moaning softly into the blankets. I could hear the slick sound of him fisting his cock, which just spurred me on. It didn't take me long to realize he'd lubed up his cock. He removed his fingers and positioned himself at my ass, pushing just enough to break through that barrier of muscles as he slowly slid inside of me.

"Fuck, Angel," he groaned once he was completely inside, holding himself there for me to adjust.

He reached around to my clit, working the bundle of nerves until I was moaning and thrusting my hips back, causing a moan to fall from his lips.

"Such a good little fucking slut for me, Angel." He praised as he thrust into my ass, his fingers never leaving my clit.

He worked me until I was about to explode, his hips faltering slightly as he reached his own release, "Come for me, baby girl," He groaned out as he slammed into me one last time.

It was the only thing I needed to topple over that edge of pleasure, screaming his name into the sheets as the hardest orgasm I'd ever had washed over me.

It was well after lunchtime when Damon finally left me. He had left a pair of his spandex boxers and a black band shirt that would swallow me in the attached bathroom so that I could shower and freshen up. Damon had taken it upon himself to go collect "some things" from my apartment. Making it clear I was staying here for a while longer.

I took my time in the shower and got some much needed time to myself, deciding to go find something to fill my empty stomach before Damon returned. We'd head to Hellfire for the night soon after he brought me my things. The house was exactly what you would think of when you thought of rich pricks with far too much money. All the white and gold had me wanting to break something. Just to add a bit of chaos to the pristine place.

I found my way into the kitchen and started putting together something to eat and a pot of coffee. After the long night I had, with very little sleep, I'd need more caffeine than usual to get through my shift tonight. I settled at the white marble-topped island with a steaming cup of coffee and a bowl of mixed fruits I'd found in the fridge.

I was enjoying my alone time until Madax made his appearance of the day. He slipped into the kitchen and made himself a cup of coffee before coming to sit beside me. When he sat down, he slipped his hand up my thigh, resting it at the hem of the boxers I had on.

"I take it you had an enjoyable evening, darling?" He asked, taking a sip from his mug.

I simply smiled before popping a grape into my mouth, "Of course, sir."

His hand trailed farther up my leg to my center, rubbing me through the thin material of the boxers. "I would hope so with all that noise you were making."

As if called by the devil himself, Damon walked into the kitchen at that moment, though Madax didn't stop his exploring hand. Glancing at Damon, I could see how intently he watched Madax's other hand as it slipped under my shirt to pinch and tease at my breast. I could feel my body tensing, and not at all in a good way. Madax took his time playing with me. His hand rubbed at my clit through the thin material of the boxers I was wearing and I had to grip onto the edge of the countertop to keep myself steady. This had become a game for him and felt more like punishment for me and Damon.

He pinched and pulled my nipple as it peaked at the attention. Fucking traitorous body of mine liked the attention even though I hated the man touching me. I stared, wide eyed, at Damon standing in the entryway. Madax moved his hand to slip into the boxers, inserting two fingers into my pussy as he worked my clit with his thumb. Last night he had been sloppy, but today he was pulling out all the stops to make me come.

Fuck, Madax was going to make me finish while Damon was forced to watch. My nails dug into the counter as my pussy clenched around Madax's fingers and a mewling sound left my lips as I came. It was nothing compared to what Damon did to me, but it had still happened and shame washed over me. Madax removed his now glistening fingers from me and licked them. He groaned as he tasted me without taking his eyes off my face. I couldn't look at either of them.

Damon cleared his throat, which seemed to grab Madax's attention. "Sir, we have to get ready for our shift at Hellfire."

I watched as he continuously fisted his hands at his sides. While he sounded calm and collected, his body language was saying something completely different. Madax just smiled as he took my hand in his, kissing the knuckles and smiling at me, almost sweetly.

"I'd love to take you out sometime this week while you're staying here. I haven't had you to myself." It wasn't phrased like a question, but as a demand. I had a feeling he never gave people the opportunity to tell him no, not that he'd listen even if they did.

I smiled and hoped it didn't look like a grimace. "Of course. How long am I going to be staying here?"

I must have been convincing, because his eyes seemed to twinkle in the light streaming in from outside. "As long as you'd like. I have some meetings, but I will see you again soon."

He stood, placing a light kiss on my cheek before leaving the kitchen, patting Damon on the shoulder as he passed with the hand he'd just used to make me come. I finished my bowl of fruit and coffee, rinsing them off to place in the dishwasher, while also avoiding looking at Damon. He was still tense and I couldn't stand to look at him after what had happened. I hadn't meant to, didn't want what had just happened. It made me feel dirty and sick to my stomach. I was also well aware I wasn't just free to leave, despite Madax saying otherwise. This was going to be a shit show.

CHAPTER THIRTEEN

Things had been fairly quiet where Madax was concerned while I stayed at his estate. The weekend had been busy, and I hadn't seen Madax except in passing. In those moments, he took every opportunity to touch me, but he hadn't demanded sex. On the other hand, Damon and I spent every moment together between our long nights, working at Hellfire, and spending our days prior to work wrapped up in each other's arms around the house.

I began to actually enjoy my time with him and couldn't seem to get enough. It hadn't been my plan to spend so much time with him when I was supposed to be seducing Madax. Madax had turned it into a game where he liked to touch me in front of Damon. He was controlling and demanding, as if he was trying to rub it in Damon's face that I was his and he was the one in control. I knew it was only a matter of time before he completely demanded my time and attention. That he was going to take me from Damon and stake his claim.

Tuesday, I took extra care to get ready for my "date" with Madax in my guest room. It bothered me being here and not in a space of my own, but being in the same house as my target would make getting close that much easier. I decided on a thigh length, red, strapless body-con dress, paired with black strappy heels for a simple yet bold look. My black hair was down in long beach waves and I applied light makeup with my signature red lip that matched the dress perfectly. As I was finishing up, I heard a light knock on the door.

"It's open." I didn't ever turn to look as Damon entered the room while I finished hooking the strap of my heel.

"Are you ready for tonight?" He asked as he crouched down in front of where I was sitting on the edge of the bed to finish hooking the strap of my shoe.

I simply glared at him before standing up to retrieve my bag from the top of the dresser. Opening it up, I checked to make sure I had everything I might need: my phone, wallet, knife, and a small handgun, just in case. Damon walked up behind me then, running his tattooed knuckles over my exposed arms. Tracing the patterns and line work of my tattoos.

"I can't protect you tonight."

I scoffed, brushing his hand off of me as I turned to face him. "I don't need you to protect me, Damon. I'm perfectly capable of handling this on my own. You aren't my protector. You're just a good fuck while I do a job."

I had expected him to be hurt, or at least angry at my comment. He surprised me when he simply flashed me his crooked smirk. Within a blink, his hand was around my throat, pinning my back against the dresser. Fuck, he was fast for someone so big. He stepped closer, no longer leaving any space between our bodies as he towered over me. With his hand around my throat, he forced me to look up at him, tightening his grip slightly.

"When this is over, you're going to beg to stay with me, Angel." He said from deep in his chest. The sound was more growly than usual and it had shivers racking across my skin.

He was fucking wrong. When this was over, I would fucking disappear, just like I'd always planned. My revenge would be complete and I could move on with my life. I didn't need him. Yes, getting close to him had gotten me close to Madax, but I would have killed him, regardless.

I glared up at him as he held me captive in his arms and spit in his face, "In your dreams."

He wiped his face with his free hand, the smirk on his face turning from entertained to one that made my heart stop. It was the smile of someone who was unhinged and I'd just poked the beast. I hadn't seen this side of him yet. His grip around my neck tightened, cutting off my air supply as I dug my nails into his wrist, trying to break his hold. Nothing seemed to faze him and his grip didn't slack until there was another knock on my door before Madax walked in.

Madax's eyes traveled between us, and Damon removed his hands from me, backing up to a reasonable distance. There was a mischievous twinkle in Madax's eyes as he took in the scene.

"I do hope I wasn't interrupting." He smiled, tucking his hands into the pockets of his slacks.

Tonight he was in a pair of light gray slacks, a white button up dress shirt with the two top buttons undone and sleeves rolled up to show the ink that covered his arms. His black dress shoes were polished to the point that they seemed to absorb the light in the room and his hair was in its usual slicked back style. His salt and pepper bread trimmed into a very put together style with just the right amount of rugged sex appeal.

I smiled in his direction while running my hands lightly down my dress to smooth out any wrinkles. "Of course not. Are you ready to go?"

"Whenever you are, darling."

I walked over to him, linking my arm with his as he led me out of the room. I wasn't even going to give Damon the satisfaction of glancing back at him.

Dinner was at one of the nicest places I'd ever been in. One of those places where you couldn't get in without a reservation months in advance. I was glad I had opted for a nicer dress, because even in that I felt slightly under dressed. From the looks of things, it was a fancy French place, and the menu wasn't even in English.

Madax took the chance to order an expensive bottle of wine for the table and to order something for me. I was surprised to learn that he spoke perfect French and was less surprised to find that he was a silent owner of the establishment. He sat across from me at a small round table that was covered in a cream tablecloth with a golden candelabra centerpiece. White roses rested in a small glass vase and left a light, sweet scent that mingled well with the aroma of food and wine.

I didn't have to speak much, as Madax was content to tell me all about the place and himself. I simply smiled, sipping my wine, and making small noises to let him know I was listening. The food came and went, while we enjoyed each other's company and spoke mostly about him. I was happy to just sit and listen and wasn't interested in telling him anything personal. If he did ask, I gave short answers or outright lied. He couldn't find out who I really was, but I was good at pretending to be someone else. I'd used the lies often enough in my time of working through the list of names responsible for what happened to Jessica.

"I'd love to know more about you. Do you have family in the city?" Madax asked me before taking a sip from his wineglass.

"No family. I've been on my own for most of my life." I said, taking a bite of the grilled chicken and vegetables in front of me.

"Oh, that sounds like it could be lonely for such a young woman."

"Sometimes, but I'm not alone now, am I?" I smiled sweetly at him.

My answer seemed to please him as his eyes took in every move I made. "No, you are most definitely not alone, darling."

More small talk followed until we finished with our meals and the bottle of wine. We left, deciding to walk down the streets of downtown. The streets were lined with businesses, restaurants, small shops, and a bit of everything else in between.

Madax had told me all about his business adventures, how he got his start and built his company from the ground up, how he'd lost his wife during childbirth and all the other personal things that I already knew from my research prior to seeking him out. Overall, the evening had been surprisingly nice, and we headed back to his estate, where he kissed me goodnight at my door.

I slipped into my room and gasped when I found Damon lounging on my bed, reading a book. I slipped off my heels, leaning back against the door to do so as I watched him flip through the pages of his book.

"Did you have a nice night, Angel?" He asked without glancing at me.

"I'd appreciate it if you'd leave." I said, walking over to toss my bag on the dresser. Turning my back from him as I began taking off the little jewelry I'd worn for the evening, placing it next to my bag.

I listened closely as he placed his book on the bedside table and made his way over to me. When he was standing next to me, his hands moved to push my hair over my shoulder and unzip my dress. Slipping it off my body, to pool at my feet and leaving me in my simple black lace thong. He took the chance to kiss along my shoulder and neck before turning me to face him.

"You have to answer for earlier, baby girl." He said, dragging his fingertips down my chest lightly.

CHAPTER FOURTEEN

I had spent the day pissed off about how things had ended with Angel earlier. As soon as she spit in my face, I wanted to bend her over and take my aggression out on her. I wanted to make her bleed and toe the line of pain and pleasure. Wanted to watch her beg on her knees while I brought her to the edge of release, only to deny her. I wanted to punish her.

When she walked into the room, I knew exactly how I'd get payback for the way she'd acted. She thought she'd just be able to leave whenever she wanted, but she was wrong. I owned her, whether she was willing to admit that or not.

I loved the way her skin flushed as my hands traveled down her chest to cup her breasts, kneading and pinching just the way I knew she enjoyed, as a small moan slipped past her ruby red lips. I took the opportunity to quickly lift her into my arms as her legs wrap around my waist and I captured her lips. I wanted to ruin that perfectly placed lipstick and have it smeared across her made-up face.

I carried her quickly to the bed I had prepared while she'd been gone. I pinned her hands above her head once she was pressed underneath me and handcuffed them to the headboard. As soon as the cold metal was holding her in place, she snapped her pearly white teeth at me in anger. The look she gave me only made me harder, as I thought up all the ways I could break her.

"What the fuck is this shit, Damon?" she pulled on the cuffs, but couldn't get them to budge as I pinned her legs down with my own.

"Payback," was the only response I gave her as I removed myself from on top of her, sliding off the bed.

I had made sure I could still flip her while handcuffed to the bed. Grabbing her by her ankles, I flipped her over onto her stomach before securing her legs to the bed. Looking down at her, all I wanted to do was sink my cock into her tight, wet cunt. To ensure she knew she wasn't the one in charge here, no matter what she may have thought. She would show me respect and if she didn't, I would punish her. I'd enjoy inflicting pain on her delicate flesh and watching her bleed the most beautiful shade of red.

I began unbuckling my belt and, at the noise, I delighted in the way her body tensed as she tried to glance at me over her shoulder. Removing the belt ever so slowly from the loops, I watched her pull on her restraints uselessly, before walking over to the side of the bed to lightly trail my fingers through her midnight hair.

"You look so pretty tied down, Angel." I praised gripping a handful of hair and pulling her head back to look up at me, " but I don't intend this to be completely enjoyable for you."

The anger in her eyes spurred me on as she locked eyes with me. I loved the fire in her that wouldn't allow her to back down from a fight. She wasn't afraid of me, death, or anything else. I wasn't sure I'd ever get enough of her. She was a snake and her venom was already slowly eating away at me from the inside out. I was hers and I was determined to make her mine.

I released her hair and stood next to the bed, bringing the belt down on her plump little ass. As it made contact, a loud smack filled the room, but she didn't make a sound. She simply put her face in the pillows and clenched her fists as I brought the belt down four more times until her ass was a beautiful shade of red. Once I was done, I dropped the belt to the floor. Leaning onto the bed. I rubbed the welts that decorated her perfect ass and placed light kisses along the deep red marks. The only noise to come from her was a slight gasp as she tensed under my soft touches.

Leaning back up to place a light kiss on her shoulder, I whispered gruffly, "You will learn to respect me."

She scoffed glaring at me over her shoulder, "Keep telling yourself that, asshole."

The glare didn't have the desired effect, as the hunger was apparent on her face with her wide, blown eyes. I simply smirked and brought my hand down on her already tender ass. "Be a good girl, Angel, and I'll let you come."

She bit her bottom lip instead of giving a smart comeback, "Will you play nice, Angel?"

"Fuck you."

That was probably the best I would get from her. I unhooked her legs and flipped her back over before taking my place between her thighs. Biting and nipping at the tender flesh up to the D marked on her inner thigh. She had been the only woman I'd ever felt the need to brand and just the sight had me straining against my jeans painfully. I slipped her panties ever so slowly down her legs and admired how my light touch had her skin flushed and goosebumps rising over her skin. Angel's mouth might have said she didn't want me, but her body was a completely different story.

I descended on her glistening cunt, devouring her until she was panting and wrapping her creamy thighs around my head. Wrapping my arms around those thighs, I lifted her off the bed to get the perfect angle as I ate my fill of her sweet nectar. Fuck, she was the sweetest thing I'd ever tastes. I wanted more, but tonight wasn't about her pleasure. She'd been a bad girl and bad girls didn't deserve to come. I licked and bit at her swollen clit until she was moaning my name and her thighs clinched tighter around my head. My Angel was so easy to please and I plunged my tongue into her wet heat. The muscles gripping at my tongue as I tongue fucked her mercilessly, slipping my hand around her thigh to work her clit. Just as she was about to come, I quickly dropped her to the bed, smiling down at her as I licked my lips.

"You fucking bastard!" She screamed in frustration, pulling at the cuffs while I simply knelt between her legs, unleashing my strained cock from my jeans.

"Such a greedy little slut, Angel." I fisted my cock, pumping it quickly as she laid there watching.

The anger in her eyes only fueled my desire as I brought myself to release. My come coated her stomach and cunt and a feeling of possession washed over me. The entire time she cursed me, but her eyes never left my cock. She was nearly entranced as the ropes of my release coated her. Once I was finished, I took my fingers to scoop up the mess I'd made and slide it into her aching center. Her pussy clenching around my digits as I pumped them in and out of her in a slow, torturous rhythm. I wanted as much of my seed in her welcoming cunt as I could force into her. She threw her head back in ecstasy as I worked to get her back to the edge of pleasure. The urge to have her come apart on my hand was great, and it took everything in me to remain in control. At the first signs of her orgasm, I moved my fingers out of her, stood from the bed and righted myself.

"Are you fucking kidding me!"

Her screams of frustration only made me smile as I walked out of the room, leaving her covered in my come and chained to the bed. She wouldn't be finding her release tonight. Bad little sluts didn't deserve it.

The night had been interesting listening to Angel scream as she fought to get out of her restraints. Things had finally quieted down just before midnight and I knew this morning she was bound to be in a horrible mood. I took my time making her coffee just the way she liked it, with just a splash of vanilla cream, and a plate of eggs, bacon, and fresh fruit. I hoped feeding her would give her pause to out right murdering me.

I opened the door to see her exactly as I'd left her. My dick was hard just seeing her naked body strapped to the bed as she glared out the window at the streams of morning light filtering into the room. She didn't look at me as I placed the tray of food and coffee on the bedside table.

"If you'll play nice, I will uncuff you so that you can shower and eat something before we leave for work today."

She nodded her head and continued to not look at me. That was probably the best response I would get. I fished the key from my pocket and made quick work of uncuffing each of her wrists. A mix of guilt and pride slammed into my stomach as I caught sight of the raw, red marks the cuffs had left on her from her struggles. I wasn't stupid enough to touch her yet, so I backed up as soon as she was free and sat at the foot of the bed. She said nothing as she climbed out of the bed and headed to the attached

bathroom, slamming the door behind her. She was going to

be a pleasure being around today.

CHAPTER FIFTEEN

Angel

I couldn't believe he had left me handcuffed to the bed all night long. My arms were sore and stiff from being held above my head, and I was exhausted. I had no idea how hard it would be to rest while restrained in a bed like that. With everything feeling so sore, I took my time in the shower just letting the hot water soothe my aching muscles.

Once I was out of the shower, I wrapped myself in a white silk robe, wrapped my hair in a towel, and made my way back into the room. Thankfully, Damon wasn't anywhere in sight, so I plopped down on the bed and pulled the coffee and plate of food closer to me. I was surprised to find the coffee still hot after my long shower, but thought nothing of it as I downed the cup.

Once my belly was full, I felt even more exhausted than I had in the shower. There was plenty of time before I had to be ready for my shift to get a little extra rest. I placed my empty mug and plate on the bedside table and drifted off to sleep.

Things were fairly busy, considering it was a Wednesday night. Zack, Cherry, and I were running from place to place, trying to make sure everyone had what they needed. According to some I had spoken to, a business convention was in town. With this being one of the hottest clubs in the city, they decided to all come here. While I was still feeling tired, I wasn't complaining when an attractive businessman tipped me a couple hundred at the end of the night.

Closing time was just 30 minutes away, so I decided to rush some things to the back storage room. On my way there, I heard a muffled scream from one of the back hallways leading to the bathrooms. I sat the box of bottles I'd been carrying on the floor and pulled my knife from its holster as I made my way towards where I'd heard the scream.

Rounding the corner, I came face to face with a man, pinning Cherry to the wall with his hand, working frantically to get her pants down her hips. Tears were running down her face as she struggled in vain to get the man off her. I inched up behind the guy as Cherry watched me with wide eyes.

"I'd get my hands off her if I were you, asshole." I said with venom dripping from my words. My knife was held to his jugular, drawing just the slightest bit of blood.

"You fucking bitch," He growled while backing away from Cherry.

I walked with him, never removing the blade from his throat until I could put myself in the space between them. He simply glared at me as he put his unremarkable dick back into his pants. From the looks of the beer gut and wrinkles, I had to say he was in his mid-sixties, which just made me want to hurt him more.

"Get the fuck out of here before I decide the world would be better off without you in it." I seethed.

"She isn't fucking worth my time, anyway." He scoffed and walked back towards the main room.

As soon as he was out of sight, I turned around and took a crying Cherry into my arms. No one fucking deserved that shit, especially not this sweet woman I'd come to know while working here. I simply held her while she cried, shushing her while I ran my fingers through her tangled blonde hair until she calmed down.

"Thank you so much. I don't know what he would have done if you hadn't shown up." She sniffled while wiping her tear-stained face on the sleeve of her black t-shirt.

I grabbed her face gently, forcing her to look at me. "There's no reason to thank me. No one deserves something like that to happen to them. Are you gonna be alright?"

She nodded her head, hiccuping the last of her dying sobs.

"Do you have somewhere to stay tonight where you won't be alone? I'd hate for that fucker to get any ideas and try anything while you're leaving tonight?"

"Not really. Dimitri is away on a business trip until Monday. It would just be me at home. I don't want to force Zack to come stay with me. He'd be far too protective and ask too many questions." She said, looking up at me with wide, fearful eyes.

I nodded, taking her into my arms again. "That's okay. You can stay with me at my place until he gets back."

I took her into the bathroom to help her get cleaned up. Once she was feeling a bit more like herself, we made our way to the front and let Zack know what had happened. He became the protective brother Cherry had said he would be, but with some reassurance he was fine with her staying with me until Dimitri was back in town. I grabbed mine and Cherry's things from the bar cubby and we headed back to my place.

Once we were inside my apartment, I quickly grabbed her an oversized t-shirt to change into after a shower, got her set up on the bed, and made her a mug of chamomile tea to relax.

"I know it's not much, but I promise that you'll be safe here the next few days. We can go over to your place tomorrow to grab whatever you need for the next couple of days." I said, sitting next to her with a cup of tea for myself.

"Thank you, Angel. I don't know how I'll ever repay you." She said as she finished the last of her tea and crawled into the bed.

I smiled at her, taking her mug into the small kitchen. "Get some sleep."

I cut off the lights and made myself comfortable on the couch and laid awake to the light sound of Cherry breathing. It hadn't taken her any time at all to get to sleep. I just hoped she would be okay, considering what she'd been through tonight. She reminded me so much of Jessica

with that bubbly personality and innocence. I found myself

wanting to protect her like I'd been unable to do for my

sister.

The next day, we both slept in until almost noon

before getting up to head over to Cherry and Dimitri's

place. Once we were in their penthouse apartment, she got

to work packing her suitcase while I took a look around.

My apartment alone could have fit in their kitchen. It

shouldn't have been a surprise that they lived in a luxury

penthouse. I'd seen the estate and knew the kind of man

Dimitri was. She told me she felt safer at my place when I

mentioned that we could just stay here if it made her more

comfortable.

"So, what's the story between you and Dimitri?" I asked as I looked over some photos of them hung along the wall of their living room. They looked happy. Even Dimitri was smiling in some of them. They had traveled together, and it painted a perfect picture of happily ever after.

"Well, that's an interesting story. I sort of grew up with the guys, since Zack and Damon were best friends growing up. We all kinda lived in the same neighborhood until Madax got his hands on some money and they moved into that big ass house. You'd never know it, but they came from nothing, just like me and Zack. Anyway, I was the only girl, so of course I'd beg to tag along with them whenever they went off doing whatever it was teenage boys do when they have far too much time and money. I'd always had a crush on Dimitri, but being so much younger than him, he didn't pay me any mind. I went off to college for two years before I realized it wasn't for me and we met back up when I came back to town. We started chatting while he was at Hellfire for business and he eventually asked me out on a date and that was that." She spoke while wheeling her suitcase to set in next to the door.

"I'm not going to lie. I was really surprised by it when Zack first told me. From what I've seen of Dimitri, you are both complete opposites. You're so bubbly while he's so… serious." I honestly wasn't sure how to describe him. He was stoic and more robot-like than human from my few interactions with him.

Cherry let out an airy laugh that matched her personality perfectly, "He's definitely the serious type, but once you get to know him, he's nothing but a big teddy bear."

"I'll have to take your word for that."

We spent the day lounging around her place and chatting. In those few hours, I'd gotten to know her on such a deeper level than I had anyone else since I was a kid. It was nice to sit and just relax. To talk and do something normal when usually I was on my own or on a personal mission. It felt as if a weight had been lifted off my shoulders for a bit and I was just as grateful to have this moment with Cherry as she had been for my help the night before.

CHAPTER SIXTEEN

Angel

The rest of the week flew by with Cherry. We spent the days shopping, talking, and doing all the normal things friends did, all while working the same shifts for the rest of the week. Thankfully, that fucker who'd tried to force himself on her hadn't tried to make another appearance, and by Saturday night, Zack had stopped hovering like a worried mother hen. It probably helped that we were slammed, but I assured him I would keep an eye out for Cherry.

The night had been a busy one, the busiest Hellfire had had since I began working here, anyway. I was beat and just wanted to head home to my bed, or couch, since Cherry was still staying with me. I said goodbye to everyone and ensured that Cherry was okay to drive herself to my place once she was done. Zack promised to let me know as soon as she was safe in her car and on the way, so I'd know when to expect her. I made my way out of the front doors and headed down the street to where I had parked my car. Just as I was about to unlock the doors, I felt someone wrap their arms around me and a gloved hand covered my mouth to hide the sound of a scream.

My first instinct wasn't to scream. Instead, I went into defensive mode. I threw my elbow back, hitting the guy hard enough in the ribs to hear a crack in the dead air of the night. When I heard the man yell out in pain, I took the chance to sling my head back, hitting him square in the nose. He finally let go of me to clutch the bleeding appendage as I whipped around. Only I hadn't expected a second man to be standing there who had a gun aimed at my head.

"Shit, I think this bitch broke my rib." The first guy whined as he cradled both his face and side. They both were dressed in all black with ski masks to hide their faces.

My hand instinctively went to the handle of my knife on my thigh as I slid my eyes between the two. I could just make out a white van down the alley behind them and I fought the urge to roll my eyes at the irony. These fuckers were trying to kidnap me, and I wasn't down without a fight. The one with the gun was the guy I needed to take out first, as he was the most dangerous. I couldn't think about it long though and quickly unholstered my blade, launching it at the man with the gun. It hit its mark in his right shoulder, causing him to drop the gun. The other one sprang into action, making a grab for me, but he didn't make it far when the sound of a gun went off and he crumpled to the ground. I took the chance to glance quickly towards where the gun went off to see Damon standing in the shadows with his gun drawn and a cigarette lit in his mouth. I glanced back at the man I had stabbed who was screaming like a little bitch trying to get my blade out of his shoulder. Picking up his discarded gun, I walked over to it and pointed it at his head, much like he had done with me.

"Word of advice. Don't point a gun at someone unless you have the balls to pull the trigger." I said before doing just that.

The loud sound of the bullet leaving the chamber left a slight ringing in my ears as he fell to the sidewalk. A steady pool of blood leaking from his fresh head wound. I removed my knife from his shoulder with a sickening slinking sound before turning to face Damon.

"I fucking had it under control."

He just smirked around his cigarette before walking

away into the shadow of the alley that led back into

Hellfire. Rolling my eyes, I took the gun and knife to throw

into my car and headed home. I'd let Damon figure out the

cleanup. I was sick of his games at this point.

CHAPTER SEVENTEEN

Damon

I'd been keeping my distance from Angel since she had left the estate and hadn't come back. I had assumed it was because she was mad at me, but according to Zack, she had just been watching out for Cherry. There had been an incident with some asshole Wednesday night and Angel had taken up the role of looking out for her until my brother was back in town.

I had planned to give her more space until Dimitri was back in town in the next few days, but I couldn't help but to get involved when I watched her gracefully take down the two assholes who had tried to grab her. I knew she could handle it, but I couldn't just let her have all the fun.

She had been pissed about my interference, so I left her without saying a word while she fumed and left. I had other things to worry about now. Not only did I need to call a clean-up crew for the bodies of those two pricks, I also needed to call my father and set things straight about how he wasn't supposed to have his goons taking girls directly from the club. The old fuck was going to get what was coming to him sooner than he realized.

I sat down at my desk, throwing my feet up, and dialed the number for my favorite cleaning lady, setting the phone down on speaker while I went about sorting tonight's paperwork.

"Boy, haven't you learned how to clean up your own messes yet?" The shrill older woman spoke as she answered.

Her tone was that of an elderly grandmother lecturing her grandchildren for sticking their hands in the cookie jar before dinner, making me smile. "Now Rosa, you know I couldn't do a thing without your expertise."

"Damn, straight. Give me the details and I'll send the boys out to get things settled. It's a busy night though, so it's going to cost you extra this time."

"I'll double it. Thank you, Rosa."

I gave her the details and went back to finishing up the paperwork for the night. I'd handle things with my fucking father in the morning. Who knew where the fucker was at this time of night. I finished up at Hellfire for the evening and locked up. I was beyond ready to put this night to rest and collapse into my bed. The only thing that would have made it better was if I'd be sharing it with a dark-haired spitfire.

Slamming my fists down on the desk, I growled in anger at the old fuck in front of me, "I don't give a shit what you have to do. They are your men, now get them in line or I swear to fucking god I'll destroy every bastard who tries to fuck with my club."

He just sat there coolly, typing away on his computer and not paying any mind to my outburst. I wanted to put a bullet in his head, but I couldn't do it here in the office of his legitimate business, Ashford Enterprises. It was a multi-billion dollar tech company that specializes in security. I clenched my fists at my sides, digging my nails into my palm to the point of breaking skin. It was his blood I wanted on my hands the most. I needed to keep my cool, or I was going to lose it.

"I'll see what I can do." He said, dismissing me as if none of this was his problem. For fuck's sake, he didn't even care that it had been Angel they'd tried to grab.

I turned, stomping to the door, but before I could slam the door he spoke once more, words that fueled my anger and I needed to hold someone's life in my hands.

"Bring Angel back home. It's time she realized she belongs to me and can't just go off whenever she feels like it. Also, inform her that your little fling is over."

I slammed the door shut so that there would be something between us stopping me from ending his miserable existence. Someone was definitely going to die today because I needed the fucking release. It had been far too long since I'd been able to play with someone and hold their life in my hands while they begged for the torment to end.

CHAPTER EIGHTEEN

Angel

For some reason, I ended up being the first person at work today. Cherry had taken the night off to prepare for Dimitri's arrival back the next day. Walking into the club with no one else here had the place feeling overly empty and a feeling of loneliness washed over me. It was dead silent as I walked behind the bar to drop off my things and get to work cleaning. I knew Damon was probably here since the place was unlocked, but I wasn't interested in seeing him right now.

I was just about done with organizing the bar for the night when I heard a muffled scream coming from the back. It definitely sounded like a man had screamed and it had me curious about who else could be here. I was positive that the noise wasn't coming from Damon. I

tossed my cleaning rag on the bar top and made my way to

the back. Following the screams that got louder as I made

my way down the dark halls. I came up to the door that led

to the basement. Zack had informed me when I started no

one was allowed down there except for management, but

that was definitely where the screams were coming from.

The door wasn't locked, so I simply made my way down

the dark stairs, being careful not to miss a step, as I couldn't

even see a foot in front of me. Once at the bottom, I could

tell it was a large concrete space with a few doors at the far

end. One of said doors was cracked, causing fluorescent

light to spill out into the open space and the screams were

almost deafening this close. That is until it became eerily

quiet.

I inched myself closer as quietly as possible until I

was standing right outside the door. Peaking in, I could see a solid white room, covered in plastic, and blood splattered along the walls and floor. With my heart racing, I pushed open the door to get a better view, praying to whatever god or goddess would listen that it didn't make a sound. My breath caught in my throat at the sight in front of me. Damon stood in all his glory, facing away from me. His long hair was tied up into a high bun on his head, shirtless, with all his tattoos on display, and a pair of tight black jeans slung low on his tapered waist, showing off the sexiest ass I'd ever seen on a man. There was blood coating his body and arms. The sight had heat pooling at my core as I inched into the room. It was as if there were an invisible string pulling me closer to him.

There was a naked man hanging from chains that were attached to the ceiling. He was covered in blood and there was a large pool of it at his feet, which barely hung off the ground. He had obviously been tortured and by the fact his chest wasn't moving, the fat fuck was already dead.

I must have made a sound, because Damon turned around quickly to face me. Shock registered on his face at seeing me standing behind him. I could see the blood thirst still in his eyes and he tracked his eyes down my body. The action of his eyes devouring me left me feeling flushed, and I knew that if he were to reach under my skirt, he'd find me wet and wanting.

I didn't take my eyes off his face as I stepped closer and drug my fingers down his bloodied chest, "Early day in the office, boss."

A primal growl left his lips as he quickly grabbed me, pinning me between him and the opposite wall.

"You aren't allowed down here, Angel." He said in his deep, gravely voice.

It sounded huskier at the moment as his hand wrapped around my throat, forcing me to look up at him as he towered over my small frame. The thought of him being able to break me made me smile as I dug my nails deeper into his chest, earning me the most delicious groan from him. He tightened his hand around my neck to the point I knew if I pushed him anymore, I wouldn't be able to breathe.

I let my eyes travel down his body, taking in the beautiful mix of ink and blood. I'd never been more turned on at the sight of a man in my life and I wanted to feel all of him in that moment. "What are you going to do to me, *sir?*"

The innocent question had him gripping me tighter, and he took my mouth hungrily. Everything about being with Damon was primal and animalistic. He consumed me in these moments, and I was powerless to stop him, didn't want to. I wanted every part of him and I wanted him to drag me down into the depravity with him. I'd never wanted anything more in my life. That realization alone was terrifying, so I pushed it into the back of my mind as he began ripping at my clothes. He pushed me up the wall, causing me to wrap my legs around his waist. He made quick work of our clothes and slammed into my aching center without remorse. His hips thrust hard and fast into me, causing screams of pleasure to leave my lips as he consumed me. I held on tightly, thrusting my hips to meet his, forcing his enormous cock to hit me in just the right place until we were both moaning out our release.

I thought maybe that would be the end of it, but he was still hard inside of me as he pulled me down to the floor with him. He had me on top as he forced me to ride him, using his firm hands on my hips.

"That's it, Angel. Use me for your own pleasure."

It was all the encouragement that I needed as I slid my soaking pussy up his dick before slamming back down repeatedly. The groans of pleasure he let loose spurring me on as I drove us both over the edge. I took my pleasure from him until we were both a sweaty, blood covered mess tangled on the bloodstained floor.

So quickly I couldn't register what was happening. He pinned me to the ground on my stomach, mounting me from behind. I don't know how he could keep going, but his cock sliding into my ass roughly had me seeing stars as I screamed out in a mix of pain and pleasure. He took from me without any remorse as he became a man unhinged.

I wasn't sure how long we stayed down here, but I was sure that after all the rounds we'd just gone and the multiple orgasms that a good deal of time had passed. We were a mass of tangled limbs, simply laying on this bloodstained floor, while we struggled to catch our breaths.

My head lay on his chest, listening to his drumming heart rate slow as we came down from our high. His fingers lightly brushed through my hair. At this moment, I was content and completely satisfied.

Following what had happened in the basement, I'd needed a change of clothes before work. Damon really had become an animal because my clothes were completely ruined. The only thing that was saved from his wrath was my skirt. Sadly, there wasn't much to choose from as far as clothes here at the club. Damon had offered me an oversized shirt he had in his office and we had taken the time to clean up in a shower that he had downstairs. We made our way back up to open the club for the night once we were bathed of the blood and smell of sex. Nothing was said between us about what I had seen down in the basement or what had happened between us. It was probably best that we let it go.

The night was a slow one with just Zack and me working the bar with our couple of usual who just sort of hung around every night. It seemed like time was dragging on and I couldn't help when my eyes would roam to watch Damon if he was at the bar or on the floor mingling with the customers. My head really wasn't in the game today.

"So, what's the deal between you two?" Zack spoke right into my ear, causing me to jump.

"What the fuck Zack?" I squealed, backing away from him so that I could face him.

A wide smile spread across his face as he laughed at my expense and I smacked him across the back of the head lightly.

"Alright asshole, what do you want?" I said, rolling my eyes and going back to finishing the drink I was working on.

"What's going on between you and Damon, sweetness?" He said, leaning up against the bar while drying his hands with his rag.

I couldn't help it as I glanced back at Damon, who was up talking to the DJ. "Nothing is going on with us."

"I'm not so sure about that. You two haven't been able to keep your eyes off each other all night." He smiled, tossing his dirty rag at my face.

I caught it, tossing it to the counter beside me and didn't even bother to say anything back. If I was being honest, I wasn't even sure what was going on between us. There was definitely attraction, but was it possible it could be more than that? There was a pull between us I couldn't deny, but I refused to think it was anything more than physically. I had no intention of being one of those women that fell for a guy simply to end up disappointed in the end. I didn't see a happy ever after in my future. This world was far too cruel for that bullshit.

CHAPTER NINETEEN

Angel

Monday came and went with things slowly getting back to normal. Cherry had gone back to her place once Dimitri had gotten back from his trip and I took a much needed break from work. It was nice to have some time to myself after how crazy things had been. It felt like a lifetime had passed, when honestly, it had only been about two months since I started working at Hellfire.

I took my time off to just relax in my apartment watching crap TV and reading some books that I'd been meaning to get to. I couldn't even remember the last time I'd had a day where something wasn't going on. I hadn't realized how in need I was for a few days to myself. I ate crap food and did whatever I felt like doing. I didn't have anywhere to be or any need to do anything for someone else. It was nice to just be me. Even when I didn't really know who I was outside of the self-proclaimed mission I'd had for the past eight years. When this last job was done, I'd worry about all of that.

On Thursday morning, I awoke to a knock on my door. I was getting really sick of these weekly flower deliveries. I'd have to remember to tell Damon to stop with the flowers because it was interrupting my days to sleep in. Strolling to the door in nothing except my lacy panties and a fitted tank top, I slung the door open to come face to face with the man himself.

"I hope this isn't how you open the door for everyone, Angel." He said, trailing his eyes along every bit of exposed flesh.

I wasn't about to give him the satisfaction that he'd gotten to me by covering up, so I stood there bracing a hand on the door frame as I shamelessly eyed him as well. His hair was down in long, light brown waves today, a fitted white t-shirt that hugged his muscular chest and arms in all the right places, a pair of faded ripped jeans slung low on his hips, and black biker boots. Fuck, I could jump him right now.

"I have nothing to hide." I retorted, stepping back to allow him inside. The sooner he got in here, the sooner I could have those pants off him.

He walked inside and his enormous frame looked even larger in my small apartment. "I don't appreciate you showing off what belongs to me."

His eyes leveled me with a heated glare, but I didn't back down. "I don't fucking belong to you or anyone else."

He smiled as if he didn't believe me and started walking around my apartment as if interested in the few belongings that I had. I made a habit of not getting comfortable here because I knew it would all be temporary in the end. Once the last name was crossed off my list, I would disappear.

"You're going to need to pack up your things. You'll be living at the estate until further notice." He said in that deep voice that rumbled in his broad chest.

At his words, I clenched my fists at my sides. I knew by the hint of anger in his voice that he didn't like this either. He was simply the messenger. I knew who was trying to order me around, but it didn't lessen my anger.

Through gritted teeth, I said, "Fine."

"One other thing," He turned to look at me and strode up to me, slipping his hand into my hair pulling me flush against him, "what we've had has to end. My father is staking his claim. I don't want to see you hurt."

I had been wondering when Madax would want me all to himself, but I couldn't help the way my heart felt, like it was in a vice grip. "There wasn't ever anything between us, Damon."

He didn't waste a second as he pulled me into a searing kiss. This one was different from the rest. It was calmer and felt more intimate. I felt myself melting into him as I wrapped my arms around his neck, pulling him closer to me as we kissed. His tongue glided across my lips and I opened to let him in, moaning as he explored my mouth and our tongues fought for dominance. If this was going to be the last time, I wanted to make it memorable.

Pushing on his chest lightly, I backed him up until the back of his knees hit the bed, forcing him to topple onto the mattress as I climbed up to straddle him, never breaking the kiss. Our hands roamed each other as if we hadn't spent the last few months naked together. It was all so different compared to what we'd already shared. I didn't like this feeling. I didn't like that he was making me feel things at all.

Without warning, he flipped us, positioning himself between my legs as he kissed his way down my neck, to my collarbone, and to my breasts that were still confined in my shirt. His teeth bit at my already peaked nipple through the fabric, causing me to arch and moan out breathlessly. Taking his time before switching to give the other the same attention. He was worshiping my body in the best possible way and, for the first time; he was taking his time.

This was far from our usually fucking. We typically were frenzied and just simply at that point where things were primal. This was different. If I wasn't in complete denial about it, I would call this *making love*. That thought alone made a surge of panic wash over me. I don't know if I said something out loud or if he just knew my body that well, but he changed his pace at the same time that panic gripped me.

He removed my panties in a single, fluid motion and settled himself between my legs. He kissed up from my knee to inner thigh, to the D he'd cut into my skin. It was nothing more than a branded scar at this point. His tongue darted out to run along the jagged lines of the mark and I moaned softly at the feeling. I had never been owned before, but there was no denying in these stolen moments, I was his. I'd never admit that to anyone else, especially not to him.

My thoughts shattered as he ran that devilish tongue up my slit until he reached my clit, working that bundle of nerves until I was gripping his hair tightly in my hands and grinding against his sinful mouth. Fuck, he knew exactly what he was doing.

He was still taking his time, savoring every curse and moan to escape my lips, until I screamed as a fast wave of ecstasy overtook me. I tightened my thighs around his head and rode his face as the waves of pleasure took over until I was panting and sated. He wasn't done with me yet though, and I was completely at his mercy.

CHAPTER TWENTY

Damon

Never in my life had I made love to a woman, but here I was with Angel's sweet release on my tongue as she came down from her high. I knew this wouldn't be my last time with her. She was mine, but it felt right. It felt needed as she completely submitted to me in these moments.

I ran my tongue up her glistening cunt once more before standing to remove my clothes. She was the most beautiful thing I'd ever seen as she laid there watching me with hooded eyes. Her cold eyes were the brightest blue I'd ever seen as I watched her eyes trail down to my cock. I towered over her small frame. She was so small in comparison and it had a fucking twisted way of making me want to protect her. Without a second thought, I crawled back onto the bed and fitted myself between her luscious

thighs. I kissed her deeply as I slipped my cock into her

tight pussy and groaned at the feeling of her wrapped

around me. So wet and so warm. She was mine.

I pumped my hips in a slow, leisurely pace as I

made love to this beautiful woman. There was nothing

rough or primal about this as I pushed her knees to her

chest, forcing myself deeper and giving her the friction

she'd need to come, even at my slow pace. I wanted her to

feel all of me and know who it was she belonged to. She

needed to know that she was cared for, even while locked

in that house with a veritable monster.

Angel had insisted that I allow her to drive her car

back to the estate. I was hesitant since my father had made

it clear she couldn't simply come and go as she pleased. I'd explained that little fact to her and yet she still insisted. It was hard to argue with her with that look of determination on her face.

   With her bags packed, we both headed back to the estate and got her settled into the same room as before. She went about setting her things where she wanted, putting her clothes away in the closet and dresser. I sat on the bed in silence as I watched her make herself at home. The last thing she did was pull out a knife and a roll of duct tape from her bag and headed over to the headboard. I didn't ask questions as she taped the knife to the back of the headboard to her liking, where it was hidden. I was intrigued to know why she'd done it, but I knew better than to question her. Once she was done, she sat down on the bed next to me and began absentmindedly picking at the threads of the white duvet.

"Does everything have to be fucking white?" She asked without glancing up at me.

A quiet, gruff laugh left my chest at her comment as I stood up to leave. Before I could take a step away, she grabbed onto my hand and I looked down at her in surprise. I tightened my hand around hers and simply said, "Angel, you could burn this world down to ash without the help of anyone else and I'd simply watch in awe."

Kissing the knuckles of her hand lightly. "I won't be around much anymore. I'll be staying away at my penthouse near the bar, but if you need anything, you have my number."

Walking out of that room and leaving her felt like the weight of the world rested on my shoulders. All I wanted to do was stay by her side and keep her from having to deal with my fucked up father. I knew she could handle herself, but that didn't mean I didn't want to be there within reach if she ever needed me. With my stomach

in knots, I hopped in my car and drove off, leaving my

Angel at the hands of the devil himself.

CHAPTER TWENTY-ONE

Angel

It was so weird being in this house all alone. Madax wasn't here due to work, so it left me on my own as I searched the house and learned all the exits should I ever need them. I hadn't expected Damon to not be here, and I hated the empty feeling in my gut from his absence. Why the fuck did I feel like I needed him around? I'd been on my own for the past eight years, so I knew I didn't need Damon or anyone else.

This had all been part of the plan. To get Madax alone and earn his trust. What better way to get my revenge than to be in the same house where he slept? This would make it so much easier to kill him when it was convenient for me. I'd just need to make sure no one of importance knew I'd been staying here with him. On my walk around the house, I had hidden plenty of weapons. I hid knives and guns where only I would know their locations. Now I was just counting down the clock to when I could take Madax out for good.

As night fell, I went to the kitchen to prepare a meal for myself and made extra in case Madax came home early. I sat my phone on the counter to listen to music while I worked on the dinner. I helped myself to a bottle of red wine, drinking it as I cooked. The heat from the alcohol in my system had me relaxing in this uncomfortable space.

"I didn't expect to come home to this, but I can't say I'm not intrigued." A gruff voice said from the entry to the kitchen.

I jumped, spinning around to see Madax standing there, slinging his suit jacket onto the back of one of the bar stools. "Shit, you scared me."

He smiled as he took a seat at the kitchen island and poured himself a glass of wine. "Sorry about that, darling. What are you making?"

"I thought you might be hungry after work, so I'm making spaghetti," I said, taking another sip of my wine as he eyed me like prey, "I'm not the best cook, but it's one of the few things I know how to make."

"I love spaghetti." He said simply, his eyes staying far too long on my cleavage available to him with my low cut t-shirt.

I turned around and went about finishing up the dinner, putting it on plates, and served him his first. I topped off his wine, then took a seat next to him. We ate in silence, other than him complimenting me on the spaghetti. Once we finished our meals, I cleaned up the plates and glasses, rinsed them in the sink, and placed them in the dishwasher, along with everything else I'd used to make dinner.

When I finished cleaning up the kitchen, he took my hand, and I followed him into the sitting room. There was a large TV that filled up one wall and a bar on the opposite end of the room. A set up of matching white chairs and couches lined the room in between them. I assumed he wanted to watch TV, since this was the room he brought me to. He sat me down and handed me the remote, telling me to pick whatever I wanted to watch, while he went over to the bar to get himself a glass of scotch. He sat down next to me on the couch, pulling me closer so that he could wrap his arms around me. We got comfortable, or as comfortable as I could be, in his arms, as we sat down and I turned on a slasher flick. Slasher and horror movies were some of my favorites. Even I could admit that Ghost-face in the original Scream was pretty hot. That scene where he licked the "blood" from his fingers just did something for me. I was a sick fuck for finding murder hot.

"I'm glad you came to stay with me, darling. I didn't expect you to be so *domesticated* though," Madax whispered in his deep tenor, trailing his fingers lightly down my arm.

I tilted my head back on his shoulder to smile at him sweetly. What I really wanted to do was make him scream out in pain, but I didn't say that or let it show on my face as we settled back down to finish the movie. His hands slipped down my body, finding their way under my shirt and into my panties from time to time. Despite him being so touchy he didn't force himself on me, which I was grateful for.

CHAPTER TWENTY-TWO

My gratitude from the night before was short-lived. I'd made my way downstairs the next morning setting out to make myself a light breakfast of eggs and avocado on toast, Letting the coffee brew while I worked at the stove to cook the eggs. I didn't turn to look as Madax made his way inside the kitchen. I'd already placed his newspaper that had been delivered on the counter where he took a seat and began reading while I finished plating the breakfast and making us both cups of coffee.

We sat in silence enjoying our breakfast, but my body remained stiff being so close to him. My skin crawled and all I wanted to do was reach over to grab one of the kitchen knives. To feel it sink into his eye socket, for his blood to coat my hands. Instead I finished off my breakfast and took out empty dishes over to the sink to rinse. All while daydreaming about all the ways I could kill Madax. How I'd relish holding his life in my hands while he bleed out before me.

I was so deep in my head that I didn't notice when said man came up behind me, wrapping his arms around me to turn the water off.

"I had hoped you would come to me last night." Disappointment leaked from his words as his hand skated down my stomach and into the waistband of my leggings. His fingers found my clit and worked me in a slow rhythm.

I tensed in his hold as he ground his hard dick into me from behind. No noises of pleasure left me as I breathed through my nose, nearly choking on the smell of his cologne. A growl left his lips. Someone wasn't a fan that he couldn't make me scream or beg. With a strength I wasn't expecting he bent me over the sink, his hand fisting in my hand while his other pushed my pants down enough to leave me exposed. I deftly heard the sound of his zipper before he plunged into me. Fucking me in a way that wasn't meant for my pleasure. He took and my nails dug into the edges of the sink. The knives were too far out of reach. My eyes trailed to the plates and mugs? Could I break one fast enough and bury the shard of china into his jugular? No, that wasn't an option. Dimitri already warned me that he was working on something behind the scenes of all this. I couldn't kill him yet. Fuck!

All I could do was take it while he rutted into me like a senseless beast. His hand tightening in my hair as he grunted out his release. I hoped he would leave me to go wash myself, but he held me in place. His hand moved from my hair to trail down my arm while he placed gentle kisses on my shoulder and neck.

"I'll be busy this week, darling. I hope you'll have breakfast with me every morning." He ground against me as he spoke. His come leaking down my thighs in a sticky mess.

I couldn't speak. My tone would give me away, so I simply nodded. With one final kiss to my shoulder he pulled away from me, fastened his pants, and left me alone to clean up his mess.

First things first, a long hot shower.

Things continued fairly smoothly over the next couple of weeks. I worked nights at the club and found Madax already in bed when I got back to the estate from my shifts. To be completely honest, I didn't really see him that often, and I was perfectly fine with that. He made time for just the two of us to have breakfast. His favorite part of breakfast was bending more over the kitchen counter to fuck me until he was coming in me. He didn't fuck me for my pleasure, that was certain. Overall, the experience of living with the man I was going to kill wasn't all that complicated.

Damon had been avoiding me even at work, and I wasn't sure how I felt about that. He would only speak to me if completely necessary, but I had caught him staring at me throughout the evenings I worked. A part of me couldn't stand the distance that was between us, even though I knew this was all temporary. He'd wormed his way under my skin and I hated him for it.

Madax had mentioned wanting to take me out on a "proper date" this weekend, and I felt it would be the perfect time to go through with ending all of this. I'd need to run it by Damon to make sure I was off Saturday night and that we were on the same page. Things had to be done right. I wasn't going down over something stupid. Orange just wasn't my color. I knew Dimitri had meant it when he said he'd throw me to the wolves if need be. It was time to end this.

CHAPTER TWENTY-THREE

I was sitting at my desk at the end of the night talking to Dimitri, when in walked my favorite little play thing. She'd worn a fitted black dress tonight that left little to the imagination and all I could think about was bending her over my desk to slide my dick into her welcoming little cunt.

She hadn't even bothered to knock as she walked into my office and plopped her fine ass down in the chair next to Dimitri. "Hi boys, just wanted to let you know to wrap things up and get whatever you needed done finished. I plan on finishing this shit tomorrow night. Damon, I need tomorrow off, but leave me on the schedule as an alibi.."

Dimitri blinked at her in surprise, while I just smiled at her. She had held out longer than I thought possible since I dropped her off. I had honestly expected to find out my father was dead within the first week, but my Angel was smart and liked to fuck with her prey, apparently. I could respect that.

"What's the plan, baby girl?" I said, leaning back in my chair.

She just smiled before telling us her plan. I had to admit it was well planned out and it would be quick. The only thing she needed from us was a quick cleanup and an alibi. I'd simply say she had been at work for the entire night and we'd spent the night working at the club as usual. With the help of Jensen, I'd be able to cover us with video footage showing her in the club. The plan was set and by tomorrow night, we'd have the keys to the kingdom.

Once we were done talking over the details of her plan, Angel excused herself and headed home for the night. Dimitri sat silently throughout the entire conversation, and I was interested in hearing his thoughts.

"It's a good plan, but I still don't trust her." He said, pulling a cigarette from his pocket and lighting it.

"She saved your girl's ass. The least we can do is back her up a bit. I know you don't get your hands dirty. So, let her handle the messy business and we will take care of cleaning up together." I said, lighting a smoke.

Things could go south fast, but I was confident about Angel and her plan.

CHAPTER TWENTY-FOUR

Angel

I awoke this morning feeling refreshed and completely energized. Today was the day everything I'd been working for over the past eight years would end. I'd finally get revenge for Jessica and I'd be able to move on with my life. I wouldn't be stuck in this hellhole of a city that brought so much pain to my life.

Climbing out of bed, I made my way into the bathroom to get myself showered and ready for the day. I took extra time to shave and exfoliate in the shower, to moisturize so my skin was soft and glowy, curled my long, black hair into waves that perfectly framed my face, and applied a light makeup look with my favorite red lipstick. Today was already starting out to be a good day. I walked out of the bathroom in my black silk robe to find an arrangement of gifts laid out on my bed. It included a white body-con dress that would fall to just above my knees, a pair of silver, red bottom heels, a single red rose, and a note from Madax.

I didn't want to interrupt your shower this morning, so I'm just leaving these here for you. There are a lot of things I would love to do with you. I'll see you soon. ~ Madax

Rolling my eyes at the note, I quickly dressed in what he had laid out for me. I took it upon myself to pair it with a red lacy thong. I knew exactly how tonight would end, and I needed the old fuck salivating for me before it was over.

The day had started out fairly well. Madax took me to a nice breakfast, where they served a large spread of food along with bottomless mimosas. To say I was tipsy afterward was an understatement, but Madax was a perfect gentleman as we made our way to the next thing he had planned. We walked around an art gallery where he explained how he knew the artist who created most of the works, to the mall for some shopping, a light lunch on the pier where the restaurant, which was suspended over the rolling waves, and we ended the night at a five-star restaurant where they served an 8 course meal.

Madax had spoiled me today and shown off the type of lifestyle he could provide for me. I was certain he wanted to move things along far more quickly than I was ready for with anyone. I played along, swooning over everything he did and said. By the end of the night, we had made it back to the estate after a fairly nice day together. I'd worked my charms to get him as flustered as I could throughout the day, and caused him to tent his slacks at the most awkward moments. My plan to seduce him tonight was working out perfectly.

He took the time to escort me to my room, and I took the chance to push things in the direction I'd wanted. This was my chance, and I wouldn't waste another moment stuck in this house with this rotten man. I opened the door to my room and turned to face him.

"Care to spend the evening with me?" I asked suggestively, dragging my nails slightly down his chest. I could feel his lean muscles rippling underneath his dress shirt and jacket.

"I've wanted to feel your pretty cunt wrapped around me all day, darling." He said, peppering kisses along my neck.

"Then take me to bed, Madax." I forced myself to sound husky.

He was acting like a starved man and I could tell his hunger only grew at my words when he looked at me. His eyes were nearly black with his need. All I hungered for was his death.

He picked me up, and I wrapped my legs around his waist. He was already hard and I could feel the length fitted against my core. I kissed him to force back the gag I desperately wanted to let slip. This man was disgusting in every sense of the word. The world would be a much better place without him and his influence on it.

He carried me a short distance to the bed, tossing me onto the plush duvet. These white linens would look so much better covered in red. I didn't understand why he adored the color so much, much like this ugly dress he had me in.

I watched as he unbuckled his gray slacks and freed his cock. I couldn't help thinking how much bigger his son was. That must have been why he fought so hard to "steal" me away from Damon. The prick had an ego and while he had allowed me my fun with Damon, it had obviously pissed him off. I sat up on the bed, sliding my red lacy thong off in one fluid motion.

He stood proud and naked before me, before pushing me back onto the bed, fitting himself between my legs. He kissed me savagely as he positioned himself at my entrance. I spread my legs farther, wrapping them around his waist as he plunged into me. He obviously couldn't tell how much I loathed his touch. He didn't make me wet in the slightest. Then again, he probably couldn't tell the difference with how many girls he'd forced himself inside.

I simply went through the motions of moaning and thrusting my hips to match his pace. I could feel his breath on my neck as he trailed kisses towards my breasts. His hand moved between us to stroke my clit while he thrust his dick deep inside me. I couldn't stop the real moan from leaving my lips as my pussy clenched around him. I hated that my body couldn't get the message. That it had the audacity to like what he did to it. I only loathed him more for that fact. Every nerve in my body was wound tight as I came on his cock. My back arching from the sheer force as Madax continued to fuck me through my orgasm. I felt dirty and couldn't stand the feeling of him inside of me, making my body answer to him, and I wanted it all to end. I couldn't take this much longer. As quickly as I could, I flipped us, positioning myself to ride him.

He simply smirked up at me, "So impatient."

I smiled down at him, riding him faster. He groaned out in pleasure, throwing his head back and closed his eyes.

"Just like that, baby. Make Daddy come in your pretty little cunt."

It would be the last orgasm he ever had. I lifted myself, forcing him into me repeatedly as he bucked his hips up to meet my thrusts. He was so close, so I rolled my hips, giving him a bit more friction until he came, groaning out his release as he filled me.

At my chance, I slipped my hand over the edge of the headboard, wrapping my hand around the hilt of my knife. As quickly as I could, I released it from its holster and slashed it across his throat. His eyes flew open and bulged wide as he reached for his throat. Gurgling as he choked on his own blood. I climbed off of him while he fought for his final breaths. Taking a moment, I readjusted my white, now splattered red dress. I could feel our combined release dripping down my thighs. I really needed a fucking shower.

"That's for Jessica." I whispered, making my way out of the room. Never taking a second longer to look back as Madax gasped for the last time. Death had finally come

for the last name on my list. It was fucking over.

249

CHAPTER TWENTY-FIVE

Damon

I stood leaning against the wall, smoking my fifth cigarette within the past hour. I'd spent the night with my bike parked just in view of the house so that I'd know when it was done. Once they'd entered the house, I'd slipped inside and waited here outside Angel's bedroom door. The noises they were making were enough to piss me off, even though I knew it was all fake on Angel's part. The door opened and god, Angel was a sight. Seeing her exit that room in her white, fitted dress covered in blood was probably the hottest thing I'd ever laid eyes on. She held her knife in one hand and a lace thong dangled from the fingertips of her other. She looked like a bloody angel of death and my dick strained against my zipper.

She smiled upon seeing me standing there and extended the panties towards me. "I believe these belong to you."

I smirked around my cigarette, grabbed her around the waist, pulling her against me. "I think I already have what belongs to me right here."

I plucked the panties from her hand, stuffing them in my back pocket.

She glared up at me and placed her knife against my throat. "I belong to no man."

If looks could kill, I'd be a rotting corpse. Instead, all I wanted to do was fuck her here in this hall. Just the thought had me growing painfully hard. I slipped my hand into her dark, midnight hair, forcing her face closer to mine. I discarded my cigarette and smiled down at her beautiful face.

"Keep telling yourself that, baby girl."

I quickly picked her up with one arm and twisted us, forcing her back against the wall. In the rush, she dropped her knife, and I took the chance to kiss her shamelessly. She wrapped her legs around me and ground against my cock. Fuck, she was already soaking and I could feel the heat seeping into my jeans. My Angel was always ready for me. Reaching between us, she made quick work of freeing my cock and positioned it at the entrance of her dripping wet pussy. I needed no other invitation and thrust into her, hard. She moaned loudly against my lips and rocked her hips to match my pounding thrusts. I could die a happy man with her cunt strangling my cock.

I increased my pace, fucking her ruthlessly. She threw her head back against the wall, moaning my name towards the ceiling. She was already so close for me. Moving one hand from around her thigh, I lightly wrapped it around her slender throat, increasing the pressure slightly. I could already feel her pussy tightening around my cock. I slowed my pace just enough to keep her on the edge.

"Who do you belong to, Angel?" I growled in her ear.

I could feel her take a shallow breath. Almost like she was fighting with herself, which I'm sure she was. I slowed my pace farther and what could only be considered a growl formed in her throat. It only made my grin widen, and I bit into the tender flesh below her ear. She thread her fingers into my hair, pulling hard enough to force me from her neck. Fuck, my angel was so hot when she was pissed. I slammed my cock deeper into her welcoming cunt and a loud, pleasured moan escaped her lips, forcing her eyes to roll. I simply smirked at her and repeated the question.

"Who do you belong to?" I emphasized each word with a hard thrust of my hips. I knew I sounded demanding, but I needed to hear her say the words.

"You!" she screamed at me, digging her nails deeper into my skin. "Now let me come, asshole."

She didn't have to tell me twice. I'd gotten what I wanted. I jack hammered into her tight pussy, fucking her hard and fast. Oh, so quickly she came undone in my arms. Screaming my name as her cunt gushed around me. Angel dug her nails into my scalp as wave after wave of pleasure assaulted her, but she would find no mercy from me. I continued my hard thrusts and slipped my hand between us, massaging her clit just the way she liked it. She came again in an instant. I loved how responsive her body was to my ministrations and I planned to use her up for the rest of the night.

When I was done with Angel for the time being, I dropped her off at her apartment and headed back to the estate. Dimitri was already there leaning against the hood of his car with a ring of smoke circling his head from his half finishing cigarette. I parked my bike right next to him, cutting the engine and tossing my helmet on the handle.

"You're late." He said, cutting his eyes at me, which only made me smile.

"I had to make sure my girl was tucked in. She's had a busy day." I grinned, kicking the stand down before throwing my leg over the side of the bike to stand in front of him.

He rolled his eyes and walked towards the front door. "Grab those cans out of the trunk and let's get this over with."

I did as he said and hauled the cans of gas inside. We took our time covering each floor and the body in gasoline before making our way back out the front door. He didn't look back or say a word as he got back into his car and drove off. I didn't understand what was up his ass tonight. We'd gotten what we wanted, and he'd soon be the big man on top.

I pulled out a cigarette and match, striking it on the side of the door frame. Once I lit my smoke, I tossed the match into the foyer and the white rugs erupted into flames. I made my way back to my bike and drove a little way from the estate. Far enough that I wouldn't be noticed when the authorities showed up, yet still close enough to watch the action.

The place was engulfed in flames by the time anyone showed up. There was little else other than the foundation left once they put the fires out. I wish that

Angel could have been here to see the masterpiece, but she had insisted that I drop her off at her place. I only stayed until people were sent out to see what was left. They wouldn't find any traces of my father, so there was nothing else to look forward to watching. I mounted my bike and headed back to Angel's place, as the sun was just beginning to rise in the distance.

CHAPTER TWENTY-SIX

Angel

Damon had been gone most of the night, which gave me just enough time to pack up the few bags I could fit on my bike. I was hoping to be gone before he had gotten back, but I heard the door click open as I was throwing the last bag over my shoulder.

"Well, this wasn't what I'd been expecting from you, Angel." He said as his boots pounded the tile floor on his way over to me.

I couldn't outrun him, so I turned to face him head on. "The keys to the car and apartment are on the counter. It's yours. I won't be needing it."

His usual smug look wasn't on his face as he reached up to push a strand of hair behind my ear. "Angel, no matter how far you try to run, you'll always come back to me. You're mine."

I didn't have the heart to lie and tell him he was wrong. I admitted as much last night. That didn't mean I had to stay. I wasn't interested in a happily ever after sort of life. I had spent so many years getting revenge on the men who had hurt Jessica and now I felt hollow. I needed to figure out what my life could be now that it was mine.

Damon didn't need to know any of that, so I simply grabbed the collar of his shirt, pulling him down to me for one last kiss. We poured everything into that last kiss as his arms engulfed me, pulling me so close I felt as if he was trying to mold us into one being. The kiss was desperate and savage.

I couldn't tell him goodbye. I didn't have it in me. So I pulled away, leaving just a hand on his chest, and looked him in the eye. I hoped everything I couldn't say he knew from looking at me. With a final pat to his chest, I walked around him and out of my former apartment building. I didn't look back as I strapped my bags to my bike before straddling the beautiful machine and throwing my helmet on. I knew he was standing there watching me. So I waved my hand slightly in the air before driving off into the unknown.

EPILOGUE

Damon

It had been about three months since everything had gone down and I'd watched Angel drive off. Dimitri had taken over the business and had the fire brushed off as something ridiculous, like a gas leak. Our father had been inside sleeping when the fire engulfed the house, leaving his death ruled an accident.

Angel had been completely M.I.A., at least to me. She'd only spoken to Cherry since leaving. The last Cherry had heard from her was a month ago. She was somewhere on the East coast and she was happy. She could live her fantasy for a little while longer. I had people looking into her whereabouts. I was going to bring her back home, even if I had to drag her back kicking and screaming myself.

"You know they are going to retaliate, eventually. Our father was their biggest supporter, and you cut them off a month ago." I said, taking a sip of my scotch.

Dimitri threw a glare my way before resuming his typing on his computer. He'd been doing amazing with the business since taking over and I had to admit it seemed right that he was now sitting at the boss's desk.

"It has been a month. I don't know what they are planning, but I know it's coming. Everyone is on alert and we will deal with it when it happens."

I scoffed, sitting my tumbler on the desk. "You say that now."

Before he could say anything else, Zack came bursting through the doors. He was panting, and he seemed oddly pale considering his usual tan.

"They took her." He gasped out in a panic.

Dimitri's fingers paused over the keys as he looked at Zack with horror etched on his face. Zack had sunk to the floor just inside the door, and I knew what I needed to do.

Without saying a word to either of them, I pulled out my phone and dialed the number of the one person I knew would know exactly what to do. She answered after only one ring.

"They took Cherry."

ACKNOWLEDGEMENT

To the reader, thank you for giving my book a chance. You have no idea how much it means to me that you even picked up my book in the first place.I hope you liked it and enjoyed the world that took over my mind for the past year.

To Brittany Marois, I couldn't have done any of this without you! You've been my sounding board and the best friend a girl could ask for. I love you so much! This book wouldn't even have existed without you pushing me to write the thing. I will be forever in your debt.
PS: If you like YA fantasy you should definitely check out her book "The Truth of Lies". Yes, I'm shamelessly promoting my bestie's book.

To Whitney, my loyal alpha reader, thank you so much for dealing with my crazy ass and going above and beyond with helping me get this thing perfect.

To all the beta and ARC readers, thank you so much for giving me a chance and taking the time to read my book. I hope you loved it!

To my mom, thank you for always letting me run with my ideas and then telling everyone about my little smutty book.

To my husband, Jason. Thank you for putting up with me. I know I don't say thank you enough. You deal with my crazy on the daily and all the mess that happened with writing this. You keep me grounded when my head is up in the clouds and let me vent to you about some really weird shit. I love you!

ALSO BY HAYLEY BRIANA

COMING SOON

Love Me in the Dark
Angel in Chains (A Hellfire Novella 2)
A Hellfire Novella 3
Fall From Grace
Fall to Sin
A Darkside Fairytale Book 1
A Darkside Fairytale Book 2

ABOUT THE AUTHOR

Hayley Briana is a small-town girl from North Carolina, currently residing in Colorado. As a stay-at-home mom & wife, she needs some major self-care in the form of a good cup of coffee (or wine) and a good book. Escaping into a world of fantasy is Hayley's favorite pass time outside her day-to-day responsibilities. When she's not adulting or writing you can most likely find her tucked away in her home library.

For more info on Hayley and what she is working on please visit HayleyBrianaWrites.com

Follow Hayley on Social

Instagram.com/hbrianawrites

TikTok.com/@beautyandthebookcase

www.ingramcontent.com/pod-product-compliance
Lightning Source LLC
Chambersburg PA
CBHW040858010826
48978CB00013BA/1077